UNDERCLASS 7

UNDERCLASS 7

T. K. Williams-Nelson

Matador
9 Priory Business Park
Kibworth Beauchamp
Leicestershire LE8 0RX, UK
Tel: (+44) 116 279 2299
Fax: (+44) 116 279 2277
Email: books@troubador.co.uk
Web: www.troubador.co.uk/matador

ISBN 978-1783064-632

British Library Cataloguing in Publication Data.
A catalogue record for this book is available from the British Library.

Typeset in Aldine401 BT Roman by Troubador Publishing Ltd
Printed and bound in the UK by TJ International, Padstow, Cornwall

Matador is an imprint of Troubador Publishing Ltd

MIX
Paper from responsible sources
FSC® C013056

CHAPTER ONE

I'd never had it so good. And that's only because I had to make sure I had it good. I remember when I was sixteen and I walked in on my stepdad battering my mum. I remember him stumbling in every night, making me dart out of bed with worry.

"I'm alright son," he shouted, as he tried to steady himself.

I wasn't his son and I hated him deeply, but my mother just wouldn't leave. However, what hit me the worst was my brother going to jail, making me desperate to avoid the same path. The only person I could actually relate to about the hard times at home was miles away – day in, day out. Manslaughter. That's what the court liked to call it, but in reality it was self-defence. I dealt with it in my own way and that was by asserting my presence; something like making up for a character that was lost. I'd always been a cocky bastard and was determined to escape the life of misery I was trapped in. So, I became all I'd wanted to be: the owner of my own gym in my hometown. I finally made something meaningful of my life in my own way. It wasn't easy. Everyone has to do some dirt to get to where they want to be. Even though it practically cost me every penny I've had since being born into this cold world, the income and other benefits that came with it made it worthwhile.

By benefits, I mean the friends I've made. Six of my closest mates started at my gym nearly six years ago and we've clicked ever since. Deano, the criminal of the bunch, always wants the lads to engage in some sort of illegal activity to gain something for himself. Most of the time we find it amusing; other times, disturbing. Mason is the life of the party and can convert us into party animals any day of the week. This often brings out our aggressive side, you know with testosterone running high and all – especially in Rylo. He has a disgusting temper and a filthy punch on him. He loves to start trouble to test his strength, which obviously brings more bad than good to his front door.

Damian is a couch potato, literally. To this day, I still don't understand how we met in a gym because over the years he has become the laziest guy I know – unless the day involves drinking. His wife left him because he went into depression mode, and now we're all he really has. Justin is somewhat similar, but instead of just *being* a couch potato, he's a couch potato surrounded by females. I see him at various times during the week and each time he's with a different woman. You could call him a ladies man but that's a bit cliché. Not that the rest of us understand what these ladies really see in him. He's always coming up with his stale chat-up lines like, 'Hey babes, is it me or is it hot in here?' He's the one you can talk to about any female problems you're having and he always has the answer to hand. I suppose it's from experience, considering he gets through them like packets of nuts.

Then, finally, you have Anthony. He's always thought of himself as the outcast of the group because he has some real bad acne. I mean *real* bad. I know he found it hard being around us because he was always the one on his lonesome on a good night out, but we still loved him regardless of what he looked like. He adds that extra bit of intelligence to the circle, seeing as he's more of an academic than anyone else. At the end of the day, we all have different characters and that makes something superior – that makes up our team.

★★★★★

As the sun peered through my curtains, the thought of attending my weekly employee meeting tempted me back under my duvet. Over the past few weeks, the gym hadn't been doing so well and I wasn't ready for the news that today was most likely to bring. I moved sluggishly as I got dressed and headed to work. As I drove, I thought about my circumstances realistically and concluded that I'm too good to go under. I'd worked so hard to get where I was after the dire childhood I had had. I couldn't fall at the final hurdle now.

"Morning Foss," called Janet from behind the reception.

"Hi Jan. How's everything been?"

"Same old. Not as busy as we used to be, but we're scraping by," she sighed.

"We'll work something out. You know I'm always a man with a plan. Where's Ray?" I asked.

"He's in the back room," she said as her voice trailed off to greet another customer.

I walked through a cloud of sweat as men and women worked hard for their summer bodies.

"Ray!" I shouted from the entrance of the back room. As he walked out, he had all the books ready and waiting for us to assess the week's damage.

"It doesn't look good, Foss. This week we're down another

3% and if we keep hemorrhaging money at this rate, we're going to be bankrupt in less than twelve months."

"No, we can't be. This gym is the best of the best. We have customers here every day."

"We aren't running as well as we used to. Times have changed but you don't want any changes to be made to keep up with the times. You don't want to hire any new staff or take on any promotion ideas from anyone. This was bound to happen sooner or later," Ray emphasised.

"Alright, I'll get the money together and we'll make a start on getting things back on track. How much are we talking to get us out of this hole? I'm sure I can find it from somewhere within a few months," I boasted uncertainly.

"Foss, we're talking nearly fifty grand if you're serious about things. I mean, first of all we need a refurbishment – something to appeal to everyone. We need to set up a promotion strategy to actually bring new people in and we need more full-time staff. With such a big establishment, twelve of us can't cover everything."

"Don't worry, I'll get the funds," I said hesitantly. Secretly, I had no idea what my next move was going to be. "I'll see you again next week, but in the mean time think of some good promotion ideas and we can run through them together."

I wanted to end the conversation and get all this work talk over and done with. Tonight's lad's night was surely needed.

★★★★★

The rest of the day flew by and as I headed home, I played some music to get me in the mood. I always looked forward to our random link-ups. They always happened at the right time, when one of us needed it most. It was a chance for all of us to unwind and escape reality for a moment. I got in and went in the shower. I stood there thinking deeply about what I was going to do about the gym, but then realised this was no time to worry about work – and when I stepped out, I honestly felt like a new man. A few minutes later, Deano phoned me to see where I was and what I was doing for the night.

"Foss, are you still coming to Mason's tonight? Apparently, quite a few ladies are meant to be joining us," he laughed.

I didn't have time for females and the guys knew that. They're better known as distractions and all I really cared about in this life was making money the best way I could and maintaining it.

"Yeah I'm getting ready now, so I'll meet you there in about half an hour."

With that said, the phone hung up on me without any warning. Deano had a habit of not using manners as soon as he'd got the information he needed. A short time later, I was walking to the bar with the constant thought of money on my mind. I thought the fresh air would do me some good. I tried not to think about work, but who can help it when you know something is wrong? I wouldn't go under without a fight and twelve months wasn't a long time to find a great deal of money. Fifty grand; just saying it in my head made me feel like I was drowning. Taking on investors was an option, but that would mean it wasn't only my gym anymore and I didn't know how I would have been able to cope with that. I approached the bar entrance and as I tried to walk in ahead of the queue, the bouncer raised his arm.

"Back of the line, kid!" he said.

When I looked up and he became familiar with my face,

the expression of 'just doing my job' faded and was replaced with a look of 'long time no see.'

"Ey Foss, I'm sorry about that my brother, I didn't realise it was you. You know how it is when the nights are hectic," he smiled.

"It's cool man. It looks really busy tonight. Is Mason behind the bar?" I asked.

"Yeah, go in, go in," he ushered.

People in the line got real cranky when they saw us getting special treatment, but that was the perk of having a friend that owned his own bar. When you stepped inside the club, scenery would get even the oldest granny ready to get down and party. The coloured flashing lights made sure that nobody's eyelids had the opportunity to fall. The mammoth bass circulating the room with positive energy kept the crowds happy and humble. Mason had done really well for himself considering he never took anything else seriously. He lived on an everyday basis. A free spirit, some might say. But one thing with him is that he took his business seriously. He would do anything to throw the best nightlife experiences for people to remember – even if that meant getting his hands a bit dirty. I walked over to the bar to meet Mason and the rest of guys to get the night started. As I approached them, they greeted me with roars of banter and wobbling handshakes. It was annoying when they started drinking before I got here; it made me feel the need to catch up.

"About time you arrived, taking all day and shit," slurred Rylo as he punched me on the arm.

"Ey, calm down and get me a drink," I replied loudly.

"What you having Foss?" shouted Mason over the throbbing bass.

"I think I'll start off with a glass of brandy with ice. Get my nerves going," I joked.

Moments after backing my first glass of drink, the steady flow of shots began as we planned to get white boy wasted. I knew I should have been cutting back on unnecessary nights out, but I was convinced that things were going to work out. I had a strong feeling about it.

"More coming up, lads, more coming up!" shouted Mason, swaying behind the bar.

"No thanks, that's it for me. I won't be able to walk home at this rate," mumbled Damian.

"Yeah, I think I'm gonna to call it a night too. I have a lot of things I need to think about. It's sink or swim for me now boys," I sighed.

"Oi Mason, get Zee to close up tonight and come with us," Deano slurred.

"Zee!" Mason shouted. "Lock up when the night's done. I need to go home. Get some sugar from the missus and sober up," he laughed as he threw the keys In Zee's direction.

I didn't know who he was trying to fool because Mason lived with his mum and little sister. Well, she wasn't all that little: twenty-three and beautiful, to be precise. Her name was Tina. I didn't know her all that well, but what I did know was that she was a very attractive woman.

The night was a success. I set out to get drunk and I got drunk. Mission accomplished. It made me feel better about the situation, but it still didn't give me any answers as to how I was going to get out of this hole. That was the thing with alcohol. It only supressed the problem, it didn't solve it. As we made our way to the exit, I grabbed Justin from his herd of females and propped him up on my shoulder for support.

"Yo, it's time to go. Look at you," I laughed.

"You love to kill my vibe. I was about to get, like, twenty numbers over there," he stumbled.

"Well you can get them another time because right now, you're not looking too sweet," I said, pushing him in front of me.

★★★★★

Walking home seemed to take forever in the state we were in, but it was definitely helpful in repressing my worries.

"Hey guys, we need to stop for a bit, just for a bit," said Damian, leaning on a nearby fence.

We all turned around and laughed at his wounded posture.

"Hurry up! You're not the only one who wants to hit the sack, lazy ass," moaned Anthony.

"Okay, I'm coming, I'm coming."

"So Foss, what's been going on with the gym? I haven't had a good workout in ages," stretched Rylo.

"We haven't been getting as much business as we used to and if I don't come up with some money soon, then the gym's most likely going to close in the next twelve to eighteen months. You know how I do Rylo; there is no way I'm letting my life's work go under. I'm fucking Foss Franklin," I said, tensing.

They assumed the drink was talking, but my drunken words were serious. I wasn't going to let it happen even though I hadn't come up with a plan yet.

"That's mad. I never thought the gym would be going downhill like that, but hard times are hitting us all. I'm trying to save up a bit of cash for a skincare treatment my doctor recommended for my face. Well, more than a bit of cash. Over a three-month period, it's gonna cost over seven grand. I was telling you lot about it the other day. If I can raise the cash, hopefully – come the end of the year – I'll be acne-free," sighed Anthony, unconvinced.

"You may be acne-free, but I'm the one getting all the women," laughed Justin.

"Shut up and sober up! Life isn't all about fucking women. Get a grip," Anthony snorted.

"Alright, calm down feisty," said Justin, grinning cunningly.

You could see the comment really troubled him by the look on his face, but he would never admit it. He knew we liked to wind him up because we always got the funny reaction we wanted, but sometimes the banter went too far.

"I know what you mean though. A friend of mine invited me to his bachelor party in Vegas – lots of females will be there and more booze than can be consumed, but I don't have the funds right now," continued Justin.

"Good. You love girls too much. It's about time you settled down. You can't be like this forever," interrupted Damian.

"Settle down like you, yeah? Your wife up and left you because you couldn't be bothered to move your lazy ass and get another job after you were made redundant. Don't comment," snapped Justin.

"Who are you to tell me about my own wife and our relationship? You don't know anything," Damian shouted as he stood up.

Now the drink was really talking. The inner monsters were escaping.

"Oi oi, we've all had a good night and you lot aren't about to fuck it up over some petty disagreement. None of us have the energy for that shit right now," I said, stepping in.

"I say we all rob a bank. You think we'd get away with it?" laughed Rylo.

"Or mug rich people," added Mason.

I knew we could have all used a bit of money right now, but these guys were on some extreme levels of illegal and immoral thinking. There would be no point trying to get money if we wouldn't be free to spend it.

"What would you lot say about a house?" said Deano, interrupting my thoughts.

"A house?" we all replied simultaneously.

"Down the road from my house is an old abandoned house. Rumour has it that a retired rich woman used to live there until she suddenly left some time ago. There must be some sort of valuables that we can sell and split the money."

We all stared at him blankly, then burst into mass laughter.

"You're not being serious right now! When I suggested we robbed people, I wasn't being serious. We can manage, we always do," smiled Mason.

"You're just drunk and we're drunk too, so I'm going to my house before you have the chance to come up with any more wacky ideas," I said, walking in another direction.

"It was just an idea, nothing major, so you can all fuck off," he replied defensively to our response.

I laughed aloud once more before I turned the corner, leaving the trailing banter.

CHAPTER TWO

I made it my duty to brainstorm some ideas to raise the gym's profile and relieve myself of some pressure. I didn't want to take suggestions from Ray and others for my own establishment. I brought this place to the top and I wanted to bring it to the top again, alone. A cruel mentality to possess, having too much pride, but that was me. I sat down with my pen and paper and questioned myself on what I would want to see as a customer and how I would want to be treated. Buy one get one free memberships; cheaper prices on sauna and steam rooms; bright and uplifting décor. It was all about attracting the customer; great presentation for the eyes, but affordable for the pockets.

After a few hours pondering ways to save myself from utter embarrassment and bankruptcy, I had a clear strategy of what changes I wanted to implement. Now, I needed the money – the hardest part of the whole process. That evening I texted all the lads to be at mine at ten with a bottle and a barrel of laughs. It was time to unwind and kick-start the weekend. I knew I had a lot to deal with, but avoiding the problem swept it under the carpet for a while. There was nothing better than being around the people that made you laugh the most. We were more than a group of 'friends'. We had nothing in common except for the simple fact that all we wanted to do was live and have a good time. To make the most of the life we were given, no matter how it was done.

Moments later I heard Deano, Anthony, Damian and Rylo debating on my doorstep about last night's events. When I opened the door, things were getting confrontational.

"You were the one in the worst state, stumbling all over the place and holding us up all the time," moaned Anthony in the direction of Damian.

"So what, pimple-prick? That's the whole point of a night out. It isn't a success until someone's wasted," he replied.

"Well, a 'you alright Foss?' wouldn't go amiss," I said, rudely interrupting.

We settled down and poured out a glass each.

"So where's Justin and Mason tonight?" I asked.

"Mason's at work. He said he might pass round if he can get Zee to cover and Justin's out with Alisha," answered Deano.

"Last week it was Kamisha, now it's Alisha, and he's got a Brianna and a Samantha. Keeping up with him is like trying to keep up with an Aston Martin on foot," smiled Rylo.

The whole room broke out in laughter, but it was true. Justin has never been able to associate himself with one main female. He was always getting himself into trouble because he was sweet-talking someone else's woman. He didn't learn. It was a couple hours before he joined us, but by the time he came, we were already half gone. All of a sudden, my mind went elsewhere and my mood dampened. I still had to find a great deal of money and I had no ideas. It was a burden on my brain. I was so used to being right that when I was wrong and ended up in a position like this, it was depressing.

"Why's your face hanging?" sniggered Deano.

He always tried to wind people up when they didn't seem themselves. That's how he got the gossip out of them, and more importantly, a personal insight.

"I'm fine. Long day, that's all," I lied.

As always, he thought he could make everything better by pouring me a large glass of brandy. Less than an hour later, we were all borderline drunk and making irrelevant noise with our banter.

"Cheer up man, you're killing the vibe," shouted Deano, polluting my personal space.

"I got shit on my mind, Dean. I just want to sit back, drink and think without you in my face," I slurred unintentionally.

"Wassup man, why you being so touchy tonight?" he continued.

I might as well get it in the open or they would be clueless about my random mood swings.

"Basically, I told you guys that the gym hasn't been doing well recently and it's my own fault. I let my pride get the best of me as usual. I didn't want to change anything even though I knew it was what the customers wanted. I don't take my staff's advice because I know what I'm doing," I explained.

"If you knew what you were doing, you wouldn't be in this mess, my friend," said Mason.

"I know, but everyone makes mistakes. I need to find the money within the next few months or its game over," I sighed.

"How much money are you talking?" asked Justin.

"50k. I wouldn't need it all at one time, but that's the overall cost of everything I would need to get the gym up to the standard it should be at, making the money it should be making," I replied.

"I'm sure it's not that bad. It's understandable that you don't want anyone interfering with your business, but in the same way everyone makes mistakes, everyone needs advice from time to time too," said Anthony, sipping another drink.

"Alright Dr Phil, put us all to shame why don't you," joked Damian.

He was right though. I suppose I did need advice, but I didn't want it because I thought I knew best.

"Enough about work now guys, let's take some shots so I can hurry up and kick you lot out," I grinned, holding up a bottle of Vodka.

"What about taking out a loan or borrowing some money from family?" suggested Rylo as he poured out the shots.

"I don't have any family that would go out of their way to help me. I never have. And what would I look like taking out a loan? That's more embarrassing than going bankrupt," I said, before throwing back my drink.

The burning sensation made me feel good.

"Reload the glasses!" shouted Justin randomly.

Since he arrived, he had been drinking almost silently. We assumed that his time with Alisha didn't go to plan, but you could see he was trying to control his mind so he didn't throw up all over the place.

"No, I think you've had enough. You looked wrecked," I laughed. "You lads make sure he gets home in one piece," I added as the boys rounded up their belongings.

"We always do," said Damian, slapping Justin on the back.

"Oi c'mon, you don't wanna be on your knees cleaning up his vomit now, do you?" I said sarcastically.

"Whatever man. See you later," said Damian as he helped Justin through the door.

"So Foss, obviously with you having issues with the gym and all of us having money problems of our own, I think we should all pull together and do that robbery I was telling you about. It really is a minor. We would be in and out in no time," Deano suggested slyly.

"Ah, I really don't know Dean. You know I don't want any trouble on my doorstep. It's a long shot because we don't even know if there's anything worth taking. Imagine we get in and get caught. We would have gained nothing but a jail term. Plus I don't think we're in the right state of mind to make any hasty decisions now," I replied.

"I hear you, but think about it. It's an easy opportunity," he said, catching the others up down the road.

As I closed the door, I actually considered what Deano was saying for once. Usually when his mind ran away with him about greedy little schemes I ignored him, but he had a point. Then again, there was only a 50/50 chance of finding anything of great worth that could actually do something about our money issues. The house had been abandoned, so was it really robbery? I didn't know and I didn't really want to know.

⋆⋆⋆⋆⋆

The next morning, I was greeted with a filthy hangover. I fell asleep fully clothed and was dying to have a shower. As the warm water rained over me, I again thought about Deano's proposition. If we did go ahead with this and things didn't work out as planned, we were looking at a lengthy prison sentence for something so petty. None of us were angels. We all had past convictions. But if things were to work out, we could make a bit of extra money on the side. Apparently the lady who lived there was rich and had left in haste, according to Deano and his rumours, so there must be some valuable stuff we could have moved for profit – but I still couldn't help thinking it was a long shot. If push came to shove and we did get caught, was every man sticking together or was everyone going to turn? I had so many questions and thought I might as well get the answers. I came out of the shower – wrinkled like a prune – dressed myself swiftly and phoned Deano and the lads, telling them to come around. I wanted to talk about things properly and openly before I made any final decisions about my part in the plan. I certainly didn't want to be a victim of any secrets concerning something like this. A few hours later, the hungover bunch made it to my house.

"What's going on?" Rylo said, greeting me.

The others followed, all looking like they didn't want to talk.

"What's all this about? It's too early for any of Deano's shit," cursed Rylo.

"Shut up man. Foss phoned me and told us to come round, so just hear what he has to say," shouted Deano.

He knew what it was about and I think he was happy to have a little support.

"Alright, I'm just gonna be straight with you lot. We all need money right now because it's hard times. You know my problems with the gym and we all know you got problems of your own too. Deano mentioned the abandoned house that could earn us some extra cash on the side if we plan things properly. I think we should talk about it on a level," I explained.

"So what are you trying to say? You want us to break into an abandoned house and hope to find what? It's a stupid idea and I'm not on it," said Justin immediately.

"It's not just any abandoned house though," interrupted Deano. "So many people have told me the same thing about this house that it must be true. The woman that lived there was rich. Of course we're gonna find things worth money that she didn't even know about. I think we should take the chance. I have nothing to lose," he proclaimed.

"Exactly. You have nothing to lose, but you clearly haven't considered us," I replied.

"Okay, so let's say you're really being serious about this – have you thought about if we get caught? What's everyone gonna say under that pressure? I'm not questioning the fact that you all have my back, but in situations like this, it always ends up being every man for themselves," added a weary Mason.

"I hear what you're saying Mason but you know me," said Deano. "I wouldn't intentionally put us in a position where we're gonna get in trouble. You're my boys. Foss, of course I've considered you all, but it is such a small-scale job that I really couldn't see it affecting us in any way besides not finding anything. If we do go ahead with it, things are gonna have to be planned properly. I don't care if it's a minor job. I want us to still take care. The fastest of us would go in, grab what we can, while the slowest…" – directed to Damian – "…would keep watch and have the car ready for us to go. Before we make any serious movements, we carry out a little stake out to see how the area works," he continued.

"You seem to have answers for everything, but I notice you haven't asked us if we actually wanted to be involved," said Anthony, bursting his bubble.

"Exactly!" Damian agreed. "I don't understand how you can plan something and not let us know beforehand."

"Well, you know now. Enough of the bullshit – if you're in, then we start planning tonight. The quicker we get it done, the quicker we can move on. If you're not in, then leave now. It's no skin off my nose because if we do pull this off and we strike it big, then it's your loss. Simple and straight," I said, standing up.

After hearing Deano explain things again, I had already made up my mind that I was in. I needed to do something or everything I worked so hard to build would go down the drain. I had too much motivation to let that happen.

"That means you've already agreed then?" asked Rylo.

"Listen, Deano has been our friend from day one. Fair enough he gets carried away sometimes, but if he's saying this is a legitimate move, then I believe him," I replied.

"So, what's it gonna be lads?" said Deano, rubbing his cunning hands together.

"Fuck it, I'm in. You lot are my guys and I trust you. It is what it is from here," said Mason.

"Might as well count me in too," said Rylo, followed by Damian and Anthony.

"Justin, are you in or not?" said Deano.

"I don't seem to have much of a choice, so yeah," he said, hesitantly.

"Good. I'm glad we've got this sorted out now. I think we should go home and sleep off the hangover from last night. We can kick this off around 8pm at my place," I said calmly.

"Cool," they replied as they left through the door. I grabbed Deano's arm for a brief moment and reminded him in a whisper, "This is all on you."

"Everything's cool Foss, everything's cool," he replied.

★★★★★

Eight o'clock came around and I was still feeling sceptical about the idea. I knew we could pull it off because it wasn't a big job, but I still felt uneasy. If things didn't go right, it was Deano that was going to feel the wrath of all our anger. We all knew he would do anything for money. Let's just say greed was his speciality. Moments later, I heard his voice approaching the front door. When I opened up, Deano swiftly stepped in with a large writing pad, markers and the guys had black clothing prepared for the night.

"Foss, I have everything worked out. You lot hurry up and sit down so I can run through this quickly," he said, shuffling around.

"I didn't realise we were robbing a bank, Dean. Take it easy son," patronised Mason.

"Yeah, you're taking everything a bit too serious. Eager wanker," cursed Rylo.

"Alright, just listen now. It might not be serious, but we can't afford to make stupid mistakes. It's still breaking and entering," I said, interrupting.

"Thank you," exaggerated Deano. "So, I say we carry out a stake out for a few hours in the day. We can work out where we can be seen from and who may be seeing us. I don't know if any squatters have been staying there since it's been unoccupied, so we would have to look out for them too," he continued.

"How are we going to do this in the day, Dean?" asked Justin, expecting a stupid response.

"It's on the road opposite my house, so hopefully we can get a decent view. I have binoculars and some other gear to help us out. We'll all take turns to keep a look out. After we get ready, Damian will drive up outside the house and stay as a lookout. While Foss and I go in and search downstairs, Anthony and Mason go upstairs – and Rylo and Justin stand where we enter as to keep watch from that angle. That way, we have all areas covered," he explained meticulously. "I've worked out the timing and we have approximately four minutes inside before we're in a danger zone. We get whatever we can, then get back to the car and head back to Foss' house," he concluded.

We all let out a round of laughter. We couldn't help but find the plan amusing, not because it was funny, but because it sounded professional.

"Dean, is this all you do with your time? Think of the perfect crime?" I asked.

"What! Don't you think it would work though? C'mon," he said with a hint of devastation.

"I think what he's trying to say is that you're acting excited about the whole plan. But I can't lie, it sounds alright to me," said Justin.

"Yeah it does, all I have to do is sit in the car and drive," grinned Damian.

"Lazy ass. All you do is sloth out all day," interrupted Mason.

"Well to me, it sounds decent. It's not too complicated and it's quick. I say this is the one," I added.

"Ah, thank you Foss," exaggerated Deano. "See what I mean boys, tonight he's been showing me real love. You need to learn to give credit where it's due."

"Cool, so when are we planning to do this?" asked Anthony.

"I say we do it tomorrow. Let's not waste any time," said Deano.

"Yeah, I agree," I added again.

"We meet at mine around four o'clock, then we get down to business at midnight. That gives us enough time to run through everything again, do our little stake out and get ready," Deano finalised.

We all agreed and the guys got ready to leave. From what was said tonight, everything sounded legitimate, but in some sense I couldn't help but feel bad for Deano. He had a lot of pressure riding on him. As I kicked back in front of the TV, I noticed that everyone seemed so calm about things. I thought reaction to the plan would have been blown out of proportion considering Deano always wants to involve us in his quick money-making schemes. All the same, it did make me feel more relaxed and erased any momentary fears.

Adrenaline had me up early the next morning gazing at the ceiling. Over and over again I went over the plan in my head trying to establish any flaws that could cost us, but there was nothing. It was straightforward and fast. All we had to do was stock up on some decent goods and get out of there. It was abandoned so technically, to me, it didn't seem like robbery – but then again, we were still taking what wasn't ours. Furthermore, the woman apparently left in a hurry. Why leave your valuables behind? I would think those would be the first things you remember to take. It all started to seem a bit too easy now, but I needed the money. We all did.

★ ★ ★ ★ ★

As I got my car to head to Deano's, I tried to think about the things we might be able to get. I wasn't a thief. I worked hard to get my gym up and running with my own money. I'd done my fair share of dirty dealings, but a thief wasn't one of them. This time was different though. I was desperate and I knew it would hurt my pride too much to borrow money from anyone, especially family. It would make me sick having to go to my distant relatives for a loan, when I already knew they wouldn't give it to me anyway. All they ever did was try to put me down because of how they chose to live their own lives. They're the ones that drove my brother away and allowed him to end up where he is now – rotting behind bars because he was true to family loyalty. Before my mind could retrieve the vile long-term memories I took so long to forget, I pulled up outside Deano's and whistled for him to open the door.

"Yo Foss," he said, greeting me with our usual handshake.

"You guys alright?" I asked as I entered the room.

"You look vexed. Having second thoughts?" asked Anthony.

"Of course not. I'm just a bit tired. Had a late night," I lied.

"Let's just get on with this stake out, yeah," said Rylo, grabbing the binoculars and sitting at the window. "What am I looking out for?" he shouted back.

"Any witness points, any movement in the house and, on average, how many people walk by," Deano replied.

"And how long are we doing this for?" asked Damian.

"Until we're satisfied that it's clear to go in," I replied confidently.

After a while, Rylo threw the binoculars in my lap and opened a beer.

"Your turn," he said, sipping.

I carefully seated myself at the window so that I wasn't

noticeable, but everything was noticeable to me. Now it was just the waiting game.

"So, do you have a plan B if it turns out we can't go through with this? Because if you haven't, you would have got my hopes up for nothing," moaned Justin.

"No. At the end of the day, we all knew when coming into this that nothing was certain. We don't even know if we're gonna leave out of there with anything of great value. So if you're having doubts, then go, because I don't think any of us are in the mood to go over this shit again," I said, still facing the window.

There was silence. Hours went by and nothing happened. The house looked dark and dirty.

"Deano, this is pointless. Nothing's popped off in the last few hours and it's dark now," I said.

"C'mon Foss, we have to do this properly. We can't afford to get caught for a petty robbery like this," he replied.

As much as I hated being wrong, he was right. I sighed and retained my position looking out of the window. I decided I was going to do a once-over of the windows of each room and then I was done. I looked through the windows upstairs and found nothing. I looked through the windows downstairs and saw nothing but darkness, but just as I was turning away, I saw a green flicker out of the corner of my eye. I turned back swiftly and looked through the binoculars in the hope of finding out what it was. It was gone.

* * * * *

Midnight steadily approached and nerves began to settle in the atmosphere.

"I say we get dressed and do the madness now. It's starting to get tense and I'm starting to have doubts," said Rylo nervously.

"Yeah, the more I sit here, the more I feel like I shouldn't be involved in this shit," said Justin.

"Let's just get a move on. Zee's minding the club for the weekend, so this has my undivided attention," said Mason, rubbing his hands smugly.

We put on our black attire and ran through the plan one more time just to make sure it was clear and everyone understood. Before we left, I went into the bathroom and splashed cold water over my face. I reminded myself that I was doing this to progress. I wasn't going to be branded 'Foss the failure' anymore. I looked at my dripping reflection in the mirror once more before we made our move.

CHAPTER THREE

Outside was pitch black. The roads were disturbingly silent. We sat in the car gearing up for one of the most intense moments of our lives.

"Alright, Mason and Anthony take upstairs; Foss and I will take downstairs. Damian will stay in the car, while Rylo and Justin stay on the lookout. Got it?" confirmed Deano firmly.

We all nodded and pulled our masks over our faces. That's when the really uneasy feeling settled in, but we were here now. I wouldn't say it was a 'do or die' moment, seeing how no one was likely to be in there, but it still had my nerves tingling.

"Remember we have four minutes before things may start to look suspicious, so grab what you can and get out. No dilly-dallying," Deano finalised.

I took a deep breath and cast my mind into focus mode. As we ran up to the back of the house, Deano smashed the window and let us in. Immediately Mason and Anthony darted upstairs in the dark, while Deano and I walked into what vaguely looked like a living room. Every footstep made a piercing creak that heightened the uneasy feeling I already had. The smell of damp smothered me as I forced my way through thick cobwebs and dust.

"I can't see a damn thing," I whispered, shining my torch.

I slowly walked around looking for things of worth when a green flicker caught my eye. I then remembered the same flicker from earlier and was determined to find out what it was. I walked to the back of the room and up to an old bookcase.

"Did you see that?" I asked Deano quietly.

"See what? Foss, just grab what you're taking and let's keep it moving," he whispered sternly.

I stood rigid, before moving books in search of what I knew I had seen, but couldn't figure out what it was. I leaned in closer with my torch and a small pouch fell directly into my palm. It was as if it was waiting for me. I shook it gently and it sounded as if there were some sorts of stones or pebbles inside, but before I could take a closer look, Deano jumped up.

"Foss, come over here," he said quietly.

I ran over expecting bad news, but as I looked down, I saw bags of money and drugs.

"What the fuck is this?" I said baffled.

"Our jackpot, that's what it is," he replied, shovelling all that he could in his bag.

At that same moment, Mason and Anthony joined us and reacted as stunned as I was.

"Grab what you can boys; thirty seconds, thirty seconds," Deano rushed.

We bent down and stuffed what we could into our bags, before signalling Damian to pull up. I was beyond the annoyance mark. This wasn't what I'd signed up for. We didn't know whose stuff this was, but I was damn well certain it wasn't any old lady's merchandise. We didn't know what was to come either. We ran back out the way we had come in and made our way to the car before speeding off down the road.

Laughter filled the vehicle as Justin and Rylo tried to find out what we had managed to get.

"I turned around and there it was. I didn't even have to look too hard. I called Foss over and just told him to start packing. Then you lot came down and we got out of there. My heart was racing but I couldn't believe it. I never expected to find anything like that. Any longer and the torches would have got us caught," Deano explained, fighting for breath.

"You still haven't said what you found though," said Justin, becoming frustrated.

All he did was open his bag and show them.

"Where did you find that?" gasped Justin.

"As I said, I turned around and it was just there. Talk about lucky," Deano replied.

"You said the house had been abandoned for how long? How do you just 'find' drugs and money? It must belong to someone," said Rylo with a hint of suspicion.

"Listen, why do we need to know where it came from or whose it is? It's ours now and that's all that matters," Deano responded carelessly.

"So how are we gonna split this up then?" asked Damian.

"When we get to Foss' house, we'll see how much we have and work it out from there,"

"Why you so quiet, Foss?" asked Anthony. "You should be in the mood to celebrate with us."

I spun around and let loose.

"Are you all sick in the head? We're grown men and we've just robbed someone's trap house. This was meant to be a casual break-in; get a few valuable items and leave. Now we've got bags of money and drugs which could potentially mean off with our fucking heads," I shouted.

"Why can't you accept that we just got lucky? The house hasn't been occupied for years and we so happen to take up the opportunity and got lucky. Fair enough we don't know whose stuff it is, but we should be thanking Deano, not bitching. If it weren't for him, we would all be in the shit. And think about it, the worst part is over now. All we have to do is spend," said Damian, clearly missing my point.

"This wasn't the plan and I'm sure if Deano had told us we would be running up in someone's trap house, we all would have had a different take on the matter – but fuck it, as you said, it's done now," I replied, ending the conversation.

We arrived at my house and I went straight to the bathroom. I needed to be on my own and figure out my next move. It seemed like I was the only one that had a problem. The funny smell of deception lingered in the air and I didn't like it. What if the police found out we were stashing drugs, let alone thousands of pounds we couldn't account for? Who even leaves that kind of money lying around? They didn't understand the serious difference between robbing an abandoned house that no one cared about, and robbing an unknown trap house we knew nothing about and had done nothing to prepare for. My head fell as all my questions remained unanswered.

★★★★★

After having a soothing shower, I returned to the living room where the guys had everything laid out and counted up. Deano sure didn't waste any time.

"You feeling calm now?" asked Justin.

"I'm fine. I needed some time to let things sink in, that's

all," I said. "What's done is done, so I suggest we just act normal and lay low for a while. No unnecessary splashing out; drawing attention to ourselves," I added.

"That sounds easy enough to me. Another thing, this stays between us and only us. That goes for you too, Justin. No blabbing to your women, okay?" said Rylo firmly.

"Whatever," replied Justin with complete disinterest.

"Listen Foss, I just want you to know that this wasn't intentional. I didn't mean for it to go down like this, but do we really have the right to complain? We have six bags of coke and 550 grand, my boy," Deano grinned, fanning himself with a stack of money.

"Now you can definitely fix up the gym, Ants can get his facial or whatever it is, and the rest of us can live contently and do what we have to do," continued Mason.

I understood where they were coming from, but only to an extent. It still didn't erase the fact that we didn't know what was to come. I knew myself that from now on, I would be looking over my shoulder wondering who might be looking for us.

"How are we gonna split this up? I don't want anything to do with the drugs. I say my share should be 100k and I'm cool," I said bluntly.

"Seeing as I've got the club, I can move the drugs quickly and make my money that way. You lot split the rest of the money seventy-five each and we're good to go," said Mason.

We all agreed and were pleased with what we had. I made sure I was compensated for the way I was feeling by demanding a larger cut.

"Why does Foss get one hundred and we get seventy-five?" said Rylo in an aggressive tone.

"I'm investing most of my share into the gym, the rest

would be mine. You have your seventy-five to spend on what you please. Is there really a problem?" I replied calmly.

He nodded silently. I don't think any of us wanted to elongate this meeting any longer, so we decided to call it a night and the lads hit the road. It was late and I was beginning to get a headache. I went in my room and sat on the edge of my bed.

"What a fucking day," I sighed aloud.

I threw my jacket across the room and the small pouch fell out onto the floor. I remembered dropping it into my pocket when Deano had made his 'discovery'. I reached down to retrieve it before tipping the contents into my hand. Seven coloured stones glimmered in the centre of my palm. They were green, red, violet, light blue, yellow, orange and blue. It seemed like such an odd selection of colours but they were eye-catching. They didn't look worth much but they had a memorable glow about them. I made a brief examination before putting them back in the pouch. I then headed into the living room to store away my share of the money. I knew it wasn't right, but at that point in time I didn't care. I had what I needed to stay afloat and I was ready to take off. The upcoming weeks were going to be eventful. I could finally implement the changes needed in the gym and rebuild my reputation. When I thought about things in a positive context, I became grateful for what had happened tonight.

★★★★★

Staying low-key for the next couple weeks made me miss the company of the lads. Not in the sense that I was desperate to see them, but it was rare not meeting up on a regular basis.

Deano gathered us all around his place to celebrate our criminal success with expensive bottles of champagne and a few ladies. We were starting to enjoy having money to spend.

"Thought it would be Justin cashing out to impress the girls," I joked.

"It was Justin who brought them here in the first place. We went to get the drink from Mason at the club and he came back with all this extra luggage," replied Deano.

When I went over to Justin, he was already half drunk and falling over himself in failed attempts to woo his uninvited guests. I decided to go over to Anthony, who was standing by the window, and see what he was thinking about.

"What's good, my friend?" I asked as I gave into temptation and poured myself a glass.

"Everything's good. I got my first appointment at the clinic about my chemical peel in a couple weeks. Obviously I'm not nervous, but I've done my research and things can go wrong. If it's not done correctly, it could burn through my face," he explained.

"Damn. I didn't think it was that serious. Why do you want it so much? When we make jokes about you, it's only banter. We love you regardless of your appearance Ants and you know that," I said to assure him.

"Man to man, it's not that Foss," he replied. When someone wants confidentiality, you know what you're about to hear is something deep. "You lot don't understand how it feels when we all go on a night out and you get all the girls while I sit at the bar drinking myself into oblivion. Not even the regulars at Mason's who know me inside and out would consider being with me. I'm getting older and want that sort of company now. At least if I feel good about myself, I'll be able to express myself better and hopefully find the one," he confided.

I understood what he was saying. Women never wanted to talk to Anthony. Anytime he would make a move, they would act like they had just smelt shit. He always brushed it under the carpet; took the rejection like a man. None of us would have ever guessed he was envious. That's what it all boiled down to in the end. The fundamentals of his whole situation were that he was jealous of his closest friends and felt the need to improve himself because of our company. What he needed to know was that it was cool to be different. He excelled in the areas that we were lacking in. He was knowledgeable, but I'm not talking about streetwise. He was an academic that had actually taken his education seriously when he was younger. He was cheeky but modest; didn't try to live above his means. That's precisely why we loved to hang with him. He brought something different to the table. Every circle needed someone to make sense of what we might find meaningless, to correct us when we pronounced things wrong and to be a smart-ass all the time.

"I hear you. We're your boys and we're always rooting for you. We might not show it much but that's the beauty of it, you should just know. When you're going to the clinic, I'll drop you there. Give you some of my perfect words of wisdom before you go in," I grinned.

We shared a brief moment of bromance before coming back to reality and remembering where we were.

"Now, let's stop this depressing talk and get this party popping," I said, downing the contents of my glass.

When I walked off, I looked back at him and realised that the guy was genuine. To know he had felt like that and not confronted any of us was clarification. The alcohol was flowing at a rapid pace and I started to let my guard down. Before I knew it, dawn was vast approaching and I had passed out on Deano's sofa with a drink still in my hand.

"Hello hangover," I said to myself as I sat up and rubbed my head.

The house was a wreck. The guys were either sprawled out on the floor or on the bed. A few pieces of underwear and bottles were scattered about the place. Things had got crazy and I couldn't remember half of it.

"Well, we sure had a good night," said Justin, rubbing his eyes.

"You were the first one gone, so you missed most of it," I laughed.

A heavy yawn crept up on me and I knew it was my cue to head home. I wanted to catch up on some sleep before we went out again tonight. The gym was starting to show signs of improvement, but it was still early days. I had to admit that I felt more easygoing about life. The robbery appeared to be for the best. We hadn't encountered any trouble and that was what I was most worried about. I hadn't been that happy in a long time, but there was still some doubt. Was it long-term happiness or only a matter of time?

★★★★★

I arrived home and conked out on my bed instantly. When I woke up, it had begun to get dark outside. I couldn't help but think that I'd wasted a day sleeping off my hangover. Then I thought about how everything in my life was coming together and how I deserved this time to wind down. I started getting ready to head to Mason's for a few more drinks. I knew that after tonight I would have to take a break from the alcoholic lifestyle I was indulging in. Even though I was financially stable now, I didn't want to get caught up. I still had a lot of work to do on the gym and it wouldn't look good to my customers if I was only half sober at work all the time.

Suddenly, my mind briefly ran over the stones I found at the abandoned house. It was the first time I remembered them since that night. I hadn't had a chance to look at them properly because Deano had distracted me. I got the pouch from my side table and emptied the contents in my hand. I looked at the green stone and realised that this could have been what had caught my eye during the stake out that day, but it looked too small and it was in a black pouch. It would have been impossible. I jumped out of my daydream when my phone began to vibrate. It was Mason.

"Where are you?" he asked above the noisy background.

"I'm coming to the club soon. I'm gonna have a quick shower and I'll be out," I replied.

I heard him acknowledge my response, but I couldn't make out what he said with all the noise from the club in the background. I put the stones back on my side table and went to the bathroom. I thought about who I was. I should have never doubted myself. I knew I was good at what I did; I was good at being successful. I couldn't help but be cocky because when I planned to bounce back, I always did. After the struggles I faced throughout my life to get here, I think all I had left was my confidence and my mind. I began to pick up the pace and no sooner had I got dressed, I was out of the house and in the car. Turning up the radio, I nodded to the beats as they pumped through my speakers. Music was always the highlight of my day. There was a song to relate to every situation, good or bad. It motivated me as I got lost in a world of fantasy that I wanted to make a reality. When I was younger, it was all I dreamt about: living comfortably and not having major worries that would threaten my determined state of mind. I put my thoughts to one side as I pulled up outside Mason's and planned to have a good time. Outside seemed less lively than it usually did on a Saturday night.

"It doesn't look too busy tonight, what's going on?" I asked the security guard.

"Everyone's inside already. Mason threw out the guest list, said he wanted the club filled to maximum capacity," he replied.

It didn't seem unusual that Mason wanted to have a party to remember, but throwing out the guest list and letting everyone in was something new. I suppose even though we had money, it was still business as usual. I walked in and joined the guys at the bar.

"The man has arrived," shouted a tipsy Damian.

"You lot started without me again," I sighed sarcastically.

"What did you expect us to do, wait while you slept off your hangover?" said Rylo.

"Fair enough, but I'm not a common alcoholic like you, so you know how it is," I laughed.

Whilst Mason poured us a round, I went over to Anthony to see how he was feeling. We had an interesting talk yesterday and whether it was the drink talking or what he was really feeling, it played on my mind.

"Do you feel alright, Ants?" I asked calmly.

"Yeah, I'm fine," he said, before his facial expression dampened.

"What's the problem?" I said, pushing for more.

"I got a phone call from the clinic today. They've moved

my appointment to next week and now I feel a bit cautious," he confided once again.

"You have to do what you have to do. Remember, this isn't for any of us; it's for you. If it's gonna make you feel good about yourself, then go for it."

I respected the fact that he was able to talk to me out of all of us, but it was hard for me to relate. I had perfect cheekbones, nicely shaped brows, a haircut that was never off point. And I meant *never*. So in the end, all I could tell him was to do what was best for him and only him.

"You know what Foss, I never thought you had it in you to give such decent advice," he replied, before laughing off the insult.

"Ha-ha, don't get used to it. These brainwaves won't be helping you too often when I've got myself to worry about, but if it's any consolation, I'll drop you at the clinic next week," I reminded.

He gave me a nod and we rejoined the rest of the lads at the bar. We downed rounds of shots after shots until I felt my limit coming on. It was slowly followed by Damian's, Rylo's and, finally, Justin's.

"Oi Mason, I think it's time to call it a night now," I said, eager to reunite with my bed.

"No, not yet. Why you always trying to stop the fun early?" he said, snorting two lines of cocaine off the bar surface.

"What are you doing!" said Justin angrily, dragging Mason up. "I thought your plan was to move this to club regulars, not fucking sniff the goods. You don't know what's in that."

"It's my shit; I do what I want with my shit," he slurred, before tipping a bottle of vodka to his mouth.

"How long have you been keeping up with this? How can you be so stupid?" said Damian, trying to restrain Mason.

"Alright, let's calm down because we're attracting attention. Mase, take it easy, you can't sniff and drink like this. Let Zee lock up tonight because I'm taking you home now," I said.

It wasn't up for discussion. He was out of control, stumbling all over the place and dribbling on his clothes. We'd never seen him in such a state before.

"I'm not going anywhere. What's the point of owning your own club if you can't drink in your own club?" he slurred continuously.

"Don't piss me off; look at yourself!" I shouted.

I started to fume up. Seeing him in this way was disgusting. He was acting like a long-time drug addict.

"Keep it down. You go find Zee and we'll sort things out over here," truced Anthony.

All I was trying to do was look out for my friend because he was making a fool of himself in front of all these people. I stormed through the crowd, determined to find Zee and get out of here. When I found him, I tried to make things as brief as I could.

"Yo, Zee, can you do me a massive favour and lock up tonight? Mason's pissed and I'm taking him home now."

"Yeah, sure, leave the keys next to the till and I'll grab them when I've finished up here," he replied.

Suddenly I heard Anthony shouting, "Foss! Foss! Come here!"

I squeezed through the crowd once more to the bar where everyone was gathered. I broke through and saw Mason on the floor shaking violently. Cocaine was smeared over his face and a bloody substance foamed from his mouth reeking of alcohol.

"Call the fucking ambulance," shouted Rylo to the crowd. "Anyone!"

I was in shock. I called the ambulance, then stood staring at my friend helplessly. I knelt down and tried to help him control his shaking, when his eyes crossed mine and froze – as if he was trying to tell me something but the words just wouldn't come out.

"C'mon Mase, it can't end like this. C'mon," I said, trying to hold back the tears.

At the same time, I was so angry. We warned him and he refused to listen. The rest of the lads began clearing out the club, while I stayed by him and waited for the ambulance. It was going through my mind over and over again – my last words to him. Now look at me, begging my friend not to die. When the ambulance pulled up outside, the paramedics rushed in, firing questions.

"Alright, someone calmly tell us what happened?" one asked.

"He was drinking heavily and doing drugs all night. We don't know how long it's been going on for though. We told him to stop, but he wouldn't listen and started having a seizure soon after. Blood was coming out his mouth and all his veins were just bulging out. It was crazy,' Deano explained informally.

I had to leave and stand outside for some fresh air. What was meant to be a cool night like all the other cool nights we've had, had turned into a sick nightmare all because Mason had refused to recognise his limits. It was just plain old gluttony. Moments later he was wheeled out on a stretcher and put into the waiting ambulance.

"Anthony, go in the ambulance with him. We'll follow in the car," I said sharply.

"Alright, don't be too long. Things look bad," he replied.

"I can see that, Anthony. I said I'll follow behind!" I shouted as I got into the car.

I wasn't in the mood for any talking. Driving to the hospital, I couldn't understand how the night had taken a turn for the worst like that. Mason had never been this bad and he didn't take drugs. Okay, maybe a smoke now and again, but he knew what we all thought about hard drugs – especially me. I promote well-being for a living.

"You lot, we can't fall out now, we have to keep it together. We know Mason; he's strong and he's gonna take this like a pinch of salt. Right?" said Deano, filled with uncertainty.

"That's not the point though, Dean. Mase isn't like this. Since when did he start taking drugs? Look how long he's owned the club for and nothing like this has ever happened," replied Rylo.

I drove silently as we approached the hospital. I didn't want to engage in pointless chatter. I wanted to know what was going down and I wanted to know *now*. We walked up to the hospital counter to find out where we went from there. It was then that Anthony jogged down a side corridor towards us. His face said it all.

"No, he isn't dead. No!" said Rylo, punching the counter before walking out.

"What's the verdict, Ants? How's he doing?" asked Justin, with hope in his heart.

He walked outside as he said, "He's dead."

I refused to let it sink in. "Where is he?" I said, grabbing Anthony by the arm.

"You should have seen him, Foss. Lifeless," he said as he finally let the tears stream down his face.

I let him go to have his space. This was one fucked-up day I didn't need. I began to walk down the corridor looking in each room. The guys followed and at the end of the ward, we saw the doctor standing next to Mason's body through a small window.

"Only two people in the room at a time please. Sorry for the inconvenience and I'm terribly sorry for your loss," he said before walking off.

To be honest, I don't think anyone took any notice. Deano and I went in first. Mason was lying on a slab; his skin pale and his face cold.

"My boy," Deano whispered as he fought back the tears.

"I need to know what happened. We were all here yesterday. Now Mase is left on a slab and we're left with a broken circle," I said quietly.

He looked like he was sleeping; like you could literally slap him and he would jump up in his ready position, all amped up and ready to take on another day. Deano walked out, leaving me alone. It was all too much for him. All of the memories of us together came flooding back to the second I walked away from him for the last time at the club.

"You better be looking down on us from up there. Tonight just proved life is too short," I said with a short salute.

CHAPTER FOUR

When we arrived back at my house, the atmosphere was suffocating. I had to break the silence.

"Anthony, what happened?" I said calmly.

It was only then that I realised I'd already asked this and no one was telling me anything.

"When we got to the hospital, he was in a bad way but he was still alive. Doctors took him away and told me to wait in the waiting room, but I followed anyway. He started shaking again – not for long. Then he suddenly stopped and his eyes rolled back," he said, fading out.

No one said anything before Damian spoke out again.

"So what did the doctors say was the cause? Was it because of his stunt at the club?" he questioned.

"Heavy drink and drug use; it caused him to have multiple organ failure," Anthony replied.

Again, no one knew how to respond.

"I'm hitting the road; need to get to grips with this before I lose my mind," said Rylo, walking out.

"I think you should all go home and sleep on it too," I added. "The best thing for us right now is to have some space and deal with this in our own way."

It wasn't the time for us to be falling out when we were all grieving over the same thing.

"Cool, I'll phone you tomorrow," said Deano.

"Don't do anything I wouldn't do. And stay off the drink!" I replied as they left.

I couldn't lose another friend to drink right now, or ever. I closed the door behind them and inevitably let the tears flow. I had too much pride to cry in front of anyone, not even my closest, but I had to let this out. I was confused and didn't know how to handle all the emotions I was feeling at once. It couldn't have been an accident. It had been over a month since the robbery and we'd had no trouble. What if this had something to do with it? My mind was all over the place but I needed answers. Something inside me was saying 'scratch the surface Foss', but what surface was it telling me to scratch?

★★★★★

I woke up to the noisy vibration of my phone on the side table. I didn't want to get out of bed that day. It made the night before feel more like it had never happened. I stretched my arm from beneath the warm duvet and searched for my phone.

"Hello," I croaked.

"It's me. How are you holding up?" asked Deano.

"How do you think? It hasn't even been twenty-four hours. Don't ask stupid questions," I said seriously.

"Listen, it's not only you feeling like this, so tone down the attitude. We have to keep it together and get on with our normal lives."

"Whatever. Did you want something or do you just like waking people up for nothing?" I asked sarcastically.

I wasn't in the mood for chit-chat. I had a cloud of guilt

weighing me down because of last night and I wasn't ready to face the day.

"We're coming round to yours and we're all going to the gym to have a deep workout. Rylo thought if we worked up a sweat, we might feel a bit better," he carried on.

"Sounds alright," I responded, unconvinced.

"Foss, we've been through hard times and got through them as a team – another one of those hard times is now. We take the bull by its horns and move onto the next," he reassured me.

It was so true. We'd been there for each other from the rags to the riches, through darkness to the light, but the difference was we were doing it with Mason, not without him.

"Yeah, I hear you. It hasn't sunk in yet, that's all. You lot can make your way round and I'll be ready by the time you get here," I said.

I hung up and dragged the sheet over my head. I didn't know why Rylo would think going to the gym would make things any better? It was easy enough for him to let out his emotions on a punching bag, but it wasn't the same for me. I lay enclosed in my dark cocoon feeling lost. I started to consider if fresh air really was the way to make me feel like I was the one still living. Since I was taking it so hard, maybe I needed the workout the most. I rolled out of bed and went straight to the kitchen. I wasn't your typical drinker unless I was socialising, but a shot of Russian Vodka was needed to get me through this day. As the drink fuelled a fire in my chest, I went back to my room and started ramming things in my gym bag. I grabbed my jacket and the small pouch of stones slid under the bed.

"Argh, that's all I need," I said, kneeling down to retrieve it.

The doorbell rang and in that single moment I felt so overwhelmed and frustrated. The doorbell rang again and in a rage I ran towards the door and swung it open.

"Do you lot think I don't have things to do other than wait for you? Ring my bell once and wait," I shouted.

The lads didn't know how to respond.

"We were just making sure you were up," replied Anthony.

I walked back inside and they followed behind me. All of us were so heated. You could see it in our eyes that we were hurting. I gathered the rest of my gear, took a deep breath and rejoined them in the living room.

"Don't take my mood personal. I'm feeling it hard but I think the gym session should loosen us all up and take our minds off things. Then I was thinking it was only right that we go and see how Mason's family are holding up – pay our respects and all that," I said, trying to maintain composure.

"That's a good idea; we were his closest friends, how would it look if we didn't go? Plus we need to find out what the funeral arrangements are gonna be if they've made any," replied Justin.

"Sorted. Now it's time for me to dish out some ass-whooping in my own gym, so let's get out of here," I said, walking to the car.

★★★★★

Rylo was right. A good workout was the right remedy for the way we were all feeling. On our way back to the locker room, I ran into Ray.

"I won't be coming in for a while. Mason passed away yesterday and it's been tough. I want you and Janet to hold the fort. Implement the changes we went over and just keep doing what you've been doing," I said hesitantly.

It was difficult to hand over responsibility like that, but it had to be done. I knew I wouldn't be able to focus properly and therefore work would not be up to the high standards I expected it to be.

"No problem, Foss. I'm sorry to hear about Mason though. What happened?" he asked.

"Organ failure. We had a night out and he went out of control," I replied.

I didn't want to go into details, but telling him it was organ failure made me feel as though I was lying. I knew there was something more to it.

"I'm really sorry to hear that but rest assured everything in this department will be taken care of," he replied, leaving me to attend to a customer.

I made my way back into the locker room to get changed.

"I'm gonna swing by the club after we go to Mason's. It's only right we let Zee know what's going on, so he can figure out what happens with the club from there," I said.

"Yeah, I'll come with you; nick a few bottles. It's not like anyone's gonna be drinking them for now," said Damian.

"If you do that, all you're gonna do is sit on your ass and drink your life away in front of the TV. Hasn't what happened to Mason deterred you from alcohol at all?" replied Anthony.

"What is it to you, Anthony? My darg died yesterday and you think because we've had a gym session, everything's better. It's not going away, he's not coming back and drinking is my way of dealing with it," he said defensively.

"Boys, cool off. We don't want to get into this just before going round to Mason's mum's house," said Justin.

I knew if I intervened in this conversation I was going to blow up again. There was enough tension and aggravation without Damian and Anthony arguing like two little girls. On our way to the house, I dreaded the thought of seeing his family under these circumstances. How they must have felt at that time was unimaginable. It was so sudden: no goodbyes, no last words, nothing. We pulled up outside and made sure we all looked respectable. I knocked on the door and we all stood in silence. Everyone was probably thinking the same thing: what could we possibly say? The door opened and Mason's younger sister poked her head through.

"Hi Foss," Tina said softly.

Every time I saw her she seemed to become more attractive.

"Hey. Me and the rest of us wanted to pass round and see how you and mum was doing," I said as politely as I could.

"Come in. We have a few people around for a prayer. Mum hasn't taken the news well but I suppose I have to stay strong for her," she replied.

We walked in and split up. I wanted to see his mum. I felt obliged to do so since my last words to him had been some of my harshest.

"Hey Mum," I said softly as I sat down beside her.

We called each other's mothers 'Mum' because we saw it as a sign of respect.

"Oh, hello Foss, thank you for coming. Mason always came home with his stories about you and those lot getting up to no good at the club," she smiled.

I returned the gesture and said, "I know this may be of little help but if you or Tina need anything, you can call any of us at any time and we'll be here to help. I know how hard it must be, but I just want you to know that you have our full support."

"I really appreciate that Foss, thank you. I just can't understand how it happened. Mason didn't take drugs. Well, not to my knowledge anyway. I would have known if he was. He would have looked different, acted different. I spoke to him only two days before and he seemed fine," she said, welling up.

Even though I felt awkward knowing I had watched what her son was doing to himself that night, I leaned in and gave her a hug before getting up. I didn't know how to respond to her devastation.

"I know Mum, but they say when your time comes, it comes," I said softly.

"Bad things always happen to good people," she said as I walked away.

It stayed with me as if it had some sort of significance. I helped myself to a drink to calm my nerves, then I approached Tina.

"How are you holding up?" I asked.

It was the most stupid question you could ask someone at a time like that, but I had to break the ice.

"I'm not taking it well but what can I do? He was a pain in the ass like all older brothers are with their younger sisters, but I loved him," she replied.

She started to cry and that was my cue to move in and comfort her. I pulled her close and moved her hair from her face.

"It's going to be hard. He's always around, then suddenly he's gone. But trust me, it will get easier over time," I explained.

"You never think these things are gonna happen to you until they do. I mean, when I walk in his room, it's waiting for him to come back – the messy bed and the smell of cologne. It's the little things you notice when someone's not here anymore," she said, hugging me tighter.

"Well, I'm always here for you. Anytime you need to talk or drown your sorrows with a bottle of wine you know where I am," I smiled, lightening the mood successfully.

I looked at my watch and thought it was best that I left now.

"I've got to pass by the club and fill Zee in on what's happened. Do you know what's going to happen to the club yet?" I asked.

"I don't, but I suppose I'll have to go round and sort through all his papers first," she replied.

There was no point me going all the way there for nothing, so I gave her a peck on the cheek and reminded her that she wasn't alone before she went over to her mother. I found Deano to let him know I was leaving.

"Are you coming or staying? I don't have to go down to the club anymore, so I think I'm gonna get an early night," I said.

"Nah, its cool, we'll probably leave from here and go down to the club later for a round of drinks," he replied.

I took that as a no and slipped out quietly. In the car, my mind was going at a pace faster than any time before; the flashbacks of Mason's and my good days; our mad nights out and long days in; my last words to him. It was all becoming too much. When I got home, I turned on the TV and sunk into my sofa. A long and tiring day had finally come to an end and all I wanted was some me-time. I wasn't in a good place and I knew it. One of those silly Rom-Coms was on and it made me think about my life. I was twenty-six and clearly life was too short, so maybe it was time for me to settle down. I knew if I wanted to, I could find a girl with potential – a girl with an aura that challenged my own. Then my mind ran over Tina. She was gorgeous but was my best friend's sister and I felt that couldn't do that to his memory. But then again, you couldn't help the way you felt about someone regardless of other things involved and I genuinely was feeling her after seeing her today.

Lost in my world of future planning, it suddenly clicked that I had to take Anthony to the clinic next week for his skincare treatment. Sighing at the emptiness I was enduring, I evaluated my position in life and realised I was well off: a thriving business; a pretty face and the knowledge I needed to better myself. I was still young and had a lot more to give now I had the funds. I may have been feeling unfulfilled at that moment, but I knew it would pass. Life was too short to hold back on anything. That was the last lesson Mason taught me.

★★★★★

It was 7a.m. and I was waiting for Anthony outside his apartment. Yawning, I stared in frustration at his front door.

"The one time I offer to do a good deed for someone, they take all day," I said to myself.

Hunched over my steering wheel, it was another twenty minutes before he made it to the car and the slamming door made me jump from my doze.

"What do you take me for? Have me sitting here for days when I'm the one doing the favour," I exaggerated.

"Sorry, I didn't realise my appointment was this early until yesterday. Had a rough night?" he asked.

"Not really. I kicked back to some music and fell asleep soon after," I replied. "That gym session took a lot out of me," I added.

"It's not only you. My legs were like jelly, but at least it was a chance to release some tension. With Mason gone, things seem rough, but I'm just trying to look forward now," he replied.

"That's what we all have to do," I yawned uncontrollably.

I didn't mean to appear disinterested but I never really was a morning person.

"So, what's going to be happening at the clinic today then?" I asked curiously. "Is it a thing where you walk in looking like Mick Jagger and walk out looking like Jason Statham, yeah?" I joked.

"Shut up. This is my first appointment of three and then after I'll have an assessment to see how well it's gone. It's not going change what I look like, it's just going to reduce the appearance of my marks and acne," he elaborated.

"Oh, I fully understand now. How are you feeling about it?"

"I wouldn't say I'm excited but I'm looking forward to the results. I never thought I'd be able to afford it, but now I can, I'm just taking the bull by it's horns and doing what I want to do," he replied confidently.

"I hear you, but we're here now. Do you want me to wait outside? I don't mind kipping for a few hours," I said.

"No, you go on. I'll link up with you later and you can tell me if there's any difference," he grinned.

"Alright, cool. I'll see you later," I said, rubbing his head through the window.

He was the youngest out of all of us and we felt obliged to look after him. As I pulled out to drive off, I saw him kiss the cross necklace his mother had given him before she died. I felt an uneasy feeling again but refused to act upon it in case I put him off. I didn't want to ruin this for him. I got home and lay back down in bed. As always, my mind was doing overtime and I couldn't fall asleep. My eyes began to burn with tiredness and my body felt limp, but still I couldn't relax. Moments later, my phone rang and it was Tina.

"Hey Foss, I'm just calling to fill you in on Mason's funeral arrangements," she said, all choked up.

"That was quick," I replied.

It had only been just over a week since his death.

"Yeah well, my mum wanted to get it over and done with. It's not going to be a big thing, just a few friends and family,"

"I understand. What's the plan?"

"It's on Sunday at 11am at the Bishop Church around the corner from my house. Mum thought it would be nice to have somewhere local; keep him close."

"That's nice. Well, you know we'll all be there. I'll pass the message onto the others when I see them later," I replied.

"Thank you. How have you been though?" she asked.

Her voice was so soothing to the ear.

"It's not getting easier, put it that way, but hopefully after the funeral things will start to get better. I should be asking you that."

"What can I say, Foss? My brother's dead. It's hard to see how much it affects Mum and how quiet it is without him, but I'm managing. I have to," she said.

"I can imagine. I've lost a lot of people in my life. It cuts deep, but over time it heals," I said, trying to reassure her.

She sighed, then went silent. I took it as a sign that she didn't want to talk about it anymore, so I concluded the conversation.

"Take it easy. I'll see you on Sunday and hopefully I can put that smile back on your face," I said, putting on some charm.

"Okay. Talk to you soon," she replied.

As I hung up, I couldn't help but feel warmth flow through me. I couldn't believe it; I hadn't had a crush in years. It was starting to feel as though I was sixteen again. I lay back down and smothered my pillow over my head. I was determined to get some sleep with a side of sweet dreams.

★★★★★

I knew when the day came it was going to be hard, but it was harder than I had anticipated. I stood in the mirror straightening my tie. You never think about these things. It only hits home on the day you lay the dead to rest. One day you're preparing to enjoy yourself with your friends, then the next, you're getting ready to attend one of their funerals.

I added the finishing touches to my suit and headed for the front door. Then I remembered the stones I had. I knew orange was Mason's favourite colour, so I thought it would be a good gesture to throw the orange stone into his grave as a last goodbye. I jogged back to my room and grabbed the pouch. When I poured them out onto my hand, I noticed the orange stone was missing. Completely baffled, I tried to work out where it could have got to. I knew I had counted seven when I first found them and I hadn't taken them out anywhere, so it had to be in the house somewhere. I didn't have time to ponder on the irrelevant subject of my carelessness, so I put them back and hurried to my car. I arrived at the church early and waited for the others to come up the road. There weren't many people outside and those who were polluted the entrance with cigarette smoke. It wasn't long before I saw Damian and Justin come around the corner. I sounded my horn to let them know I was there.

"How long have you been sitting out here?" Justin asked.

"Not long, only about ten minutes. I thought I'd get here early so I could talk to Tina before things kicked off, but I can't see her," I replied.

"So, what's going on with you and Tina then? Seems like Mase dying has brought you two closer together," said Damian.

"Yeah, something like that, but she's still his sister. Even though he's gone, I still feel like I would be crossing boundaries I shouldn't be crossing," I said.

"You have to live your life, Foss. I actually can't remember the last time you've told me you were feeling someone in a way more than a friend. There must be something about her, so just take things slow and see what happens," added Justin.

I took it all in but it didn't change my way of thinking. My head wasn't even straight at that moment in time, so I knew rushing things would be a bad move. Making any sort of move seemed bad, to be quite frank.

"Alright, enough sweet-talk, we need to go in now. I thought the guys would be here by now. Speaking of which, I haven't heard from Ants at all," said Damian, slamming the car door.

"Hey! Take your time with my door, hulk," I cursed.

As we walked in the church, the service was just

beginning. We found a space at the back and moments later, Rylo, Anthony and Deano came sneaking in, telling us to budge up.

"Why are you late?" I whispered.

"I completely slept through my alarm and had Deano waiting for me outside with Ants," whispered Rylo.

When the service concluded, it felt like the dark cloud of doom hovering over me for the past week was replaced with a cloud of relief. It felt like he had gone to a better place. People began to leave and I scanned the faces with the hopes of seeing Tina, but things were a bit hectic. In the end I gave up and headed to the burial ground with the others.

"That wasn't easy," sighed Anthony. "It never feels real until you're actually putting them in the ground."

"It's so true. I keep thinking he's gonna phone telling us to come for some drinks or with one of his really rubbish jokes," Deano said, reminiscing.

"C'mon though guys, you know Mason would be pissed off if he saw us sulking like this. He was the life of the party and we have to keep that legacy going," I added.

The situation we were in was going to take time to fade away but this was the final hurdle. We would say our final goodbyes and move forward. As we watched his coffin get lowered into the ground, I tried to keep a clear mind and compose myself. His mum screamed as his coffin was laid down. Tina broke down next to her. It was a sore sight for eyes. Rylo walked away, Anthony shed more than enough tears and Deano tried to keep a straight face. He tried to hide it, but I could see guilt rush over him for the first time. The same drugs he found were the same drugs that brought us here today. If that wasn't karma, then I wanted to know what was. I took one last look before the dirt was thrown on top. Anthony was spot on; it felt very much real, now Mason was in the ground.

*****

The adrenaline was high at the after party. It was exactly how Mason would have wanted it. There weren't many people at the church so I assumed things were going to stay small, but people were hanging out the door. We sat at a table switching from topic to topic over drinks.

"The last couple weeks have been a shambles," said Rylo, swirling the contents of his glass.

"You can say that again. It's like things went great for a few days, then things started going downhill from there. Mason being gone is like the cherry on top," replied Deano, throwing a cherry into an empty glass.

As the discussion went on, I sat back and thought hard. My mind was telling me I should be onto something, but I didn't know where to start or what to think. So much was going on that I didn't know which angle to take on things.

"Do you lot think this is karma? We stole for our own personal gain. Maybe this is God's way of saying we fucked up," I said randomly.

They burst out laughing before getting serious after seeing my face.

"What are you really trying to say? Mason's death is bad karma because we robbed an abandoned house and got lucky? You need to let this go Foss, look how long it's been. You've enjoyed having money to blow, so what more is there to discuss about it? It's Mason's funeral because he overdosed. End of," said Deano sternly.

My blood boiled as I registered his words, but what made it worse is that he didn't believe one word he was saying himself. I saw the hurt in his eyes at Mason's graveside and I saw the doubt in his eyes now.

"Believe what you want and I'll believe what I want," I said, standing up. "I'm going to get a drink."

As I merged through the crowd, I bumped into Tina. My facial expression screamed 'finally'. She was tipsy and giggling frantically.

"Aw, hey Foss. I haven't seen you for the whole day. Nice send-off, ey?" she said, raising her cocktail glass.

All I could do was laugh. At least she was enjoying herself.

"Can I talk to you?" I said, tugging her gently.

"What's wrong?" She said, toning it down.

"No, nothing's wrong. The service was nice and the party is just how he would have wanted it," I said, looking at all the people behind us.

"Thanks. A lot of work went into it at short notice, so I'm glad everyone could make it. What did you want to talk about?" she said, stumbling into my arms.

I didn't really know what I wanted to say, so I went in for the kill and kissed her.

"What are you doing?" she asked, wiping her mouth with disgust.

I didn't know how to respond.

"What? Isn't it obvious, Tina? I have feelings for you. But by your reaction, clearly the feeling isn't mutual, so let's call it a day," I said, walking away.

I wanted to avoid as much embarrassment as I could. I went to the bar and ordered a double brandy. She didn't need to move like that at all. She could have told me she wasn't interested, but that was unnecessary. What was I thinking? It's my friend's funeral; my mind's all over the place and I kissed his drunken sister. My thoughts were in turmoil. I walked back over to my table, waiting for the sly comments.

"So you got lost then?" asked Anthony sarcastically.

I ignored him and sat down with a thud.

"Why the sour face?" asked Deano. "If it's because of what I said, I'm just telling you how it is. I don't mean anything by it."

"No, it's not that. I've messed things up with Tina before they've even started," I sighed.

"What happened?" he probed.

"I don't even know, Deano. I saw her and tried to talk, but I froze up. I kissed her and basically got rejected," I replied. "She was tipsy – might as well just say borderline drunk, which makes it even worse."

"One thing with girls is they exaggerate every little thing when they're tipsy. Just leave it tonight and try again at a better time," advised Justin.

"I hear you but I'm gonna leave it full stop. I've already crossed the line and she's still Mason's sister. I feel uncomfortable about that in itself," I replied, feeling disappointed.

"Well, it's up to you, but personally I don't see the problem. I'm sure Mason would rather her be with you than with someone who wouldn't treat her right," said Rylo.

I agreed, but it didn't help how I felt about it.

"It is what it is boys," I said, raising a toast. "Here's to our good friend Mason. May he rest in peace and live on through us."

It wasn't long before I was wrecked and ready for the sack.

"I'm out now, and you're coming too," said Damian, trying to stabilise me.

"I'm cool. I'm cool. But yeah, I think it's that time," I replied, trying to appear in control.

"You lot coming or staying?" shouted Damian over the bass.

"Nah, we're cool. We'll get a lift down with Justin," replied Rylo.

At that point in time, you didn't need to tell me twice. Damian and I made a speedy exit. When I stood outside, the smell of fresh air felt like a blessing. I threw my car keys to Damian, knowing that driving in the state I was in would result in my own funeral.

"So what's good, Foss?" he asked.

"I'm good. Well, not that good because I can feel a migraine coming on, but I'm glad we got today out of the way if you know what I mean," I replied slowly.

"Yeah, I understand. We have to keep it together now though. More money, more problems," he said.

"I think I need to go to bed and work on things later because I'm not on the ball. I completely forgot that I'm taking Anthony to the skin clinic tomorrow morning before going to work," I said, releasing a huge sigh.

I couldn't help but think about Tina. I doubted that she would even speak to me after tonight. It was my own fault, but as my mum always told me, everything happens for a reason. Damian parked up and helped me out of the car.

"I'm alright now, you can go home. I'll phone you," I said, acting fine.

"I'm making sure you make it to your bed in one piece," he laughed.

The next thing I knew, my eyes were burning intensely. I popped my head from under my duvet and looked around sharply. There was no sign of Damian. I rummaged around for my phone and realised I'd been out for a while. It was 6a.m. and Damian had already come and gone. I had to be up in a couple hours and I was feeling demotivated. My head felt heavy with meaningless luggage as I slowly began piecing together the night before.

*****

I held my horn as I sat outside waiting for Anthony. It was his last session and I could genuinely see the difference in his appearance and his confidence.

"You're on time for once," he laughed as he got in the car.

"You're lucky. I felt like I could take the day off until I remembered about you," I said smugly.

"Last night left you totalled, both physically and emotionally. Are you planning to sort things out with Tina?" he asked.

I didn't want to go over it again, so I made my answer brief. "No point. I know everything I need to know, Ants. She's not interested."

We arrived at the clinic and Anthony hopped out of the car, trying to play down his excitement.

"I'll pass round yours after work," I shouted as he walked off.

He nodded and disappeared through the automatic doors. I drove to work thinking about the fast lane I've been in for the last few months; so many ups and downs in such a small space of time. I reached into my desk drawer once I'd reached the gym and pulled out a small picture of my mum. She was the reason behind me still rolling on – the fuel of my fire. If only she was here so I could show her how much I appreciated what she'd done for me all those years ago. My past began to seep back into the present as I evaluated how I came to be where I was. I shouldn't have to miss my mum because she should have been here. Janet walked into my office with the books, distracting me from disturbing thoughts.

"Sorry to scare you," she smiled when she saw me jump.

"Oh no, it's fine. I was daydreaming. How have things been working out while I've been gone?" I asked.

"Things are on the up. We've launched the new memberships and promotions. The gym's getting its very own facelift next week as well," she joked.

It was some much-needed good news.

"That's great. You and Ray have been holding things down for me and I'm grateful. This month I'm giving you both a bonus and a pay rise for your work," I said, hoping a good deed would make me feel more fulfilled.

I also believed that treating your employees well made their performance more efficient.

"Thank you, Foss. I'll let Ray know," she said, closing the door behind her.

I looked through the books and was relieved to see we were no longer haemorrhaging money. I got on with some paperwork, before deciding that I'd had enough for today. I wanted to go home and relax, but I had to go to Anthony's and see how he was. For a moment I contemplated my next move until I made up my mind and drove to Anthony's house. I wasn't planning to stay long. I just wanted to go home and wind down. My phone rang and I saw it was Tina. I threw the phone on the passenger seat, using driving as an excuse not to answer. What more did she have to say? I pulled up outside Anthony's and called her back.

"Hey," she said submissively. "Are you alright to talk?"

"Yeah, what's good?" I replied bluntly. My pride couldn't take any more rejection.

"I'm sorry. From what I remember, I owe you an apology."

"You don't. Better to set me straight, than leave me hanging onto false hope," I replied.

"I didn't set you straight; you just caught me off guard, that's all. It was my brother's funeral, Foss, that was not what I was expecting. Talk about picking moments," she said with sarcasm.

"So, what's that meant to mean? I know I shouldn't have kissed you, fair enough. But you reacted with such disgust. Maybe it was the drink, maybe it wasn't, but either way I got the message and this explanation is unnecessary."

She sighed heavily. "I don't know what it was, but what I do know is I genuinely like you. Since you and Mase became friends, I always had a little soft spot, but you were my brother's friend and I thought he wouldn't approve. Thinking about it now, Mase would rather me be happy than be with someone who isn't willing to treat me right; like a woman, not some sex machine."

A smile secretly formed across my face as I listened. Maybe she was better off with me. I would never hurt her out of respect for Mason. Not to mention the fact that no one had made me feel like that in a long time, so I knew it and she were real for me. But then again, it was too soon. Was it the grief talking? Did she need someone to fill in the gap where she felt something was missing? It still didn't explain why when I kissed her, you would think I'd just given her rabies.

"You know how I feel about you, but let's just take each day as it comes," I suggested.

Easing into things was the best way to go right now.

"Sounds like a plan," she replied.

"How about you come over and see me later? We can relax with a bottle of wine. I've had a long day at work and I think a drink and some company is necessary," I said.

"Yeah, that would be nice. I'm going to the club first to sort out Mason's paperwork, so call me later," she replied.

"Alright. Well I'm at Anthony's now, so I'm gonna chill with him for a while, go home, then come to get you," I said, getting out of the car.

Before I got any response, my battery died. Mildly annoyed, I rang Anthony's doorbell and waited… and waited… and waited.

"Is this guy trying to take the piss?" I said to myself aloud. "Anthony!" I shouted through the letterbox.

I knew he was in because he text me when he got back home. I got no answer. I looked through the window trying to make out what he was doing, when I saw him slumped over his counter.

"Anthony!" I shouted for a second time.

I saw no movement whatsoever. My first instinct was to get inside, so I kicked the door clean off the hinges. I ran towards him repeating his name while I got him onto the sofa. His face was an odd colour and I couldn't find a pulse. I phoned the ambulance and waited.

"No, no, no," I repeated, pacing up and down.

I'd just saw him that morning and now he was on death's door. Something wasn't right. The ambulance arrived and I explained what happened.

"I took him to the skin clinic this morning and he was fine. I already made plans with him to come around after work and he text me to let me know when he got in. I came here and found him slumped over the counter," I said, feeling as though I was telling a story.

Thing's didn't feel real. They rushed around leaving me confused as to what was going on. I went outside to call the guys, but I couldn't get through to Damian and Deano. I knew Rylo and Justin were out of the area, but I tried anyway. No sooner had I tried to call them, Damian and Deano came running up the road at the sight of the ambulance and the emerging crowd.

"What happened?" they asked, panting forcefully.

"I think he's dead," I replied, monotone. "I came by after work and found him unconscious. I couldn't find a pulse and the paramedics refuse to tell me anything, so I'm just in the dark right now."

Deano ran inside, while Damian still tried to catch his breath.

"How? He was fine yesterday," he said.

"And I took him to the skin clinic this morning and he was fine then too, so what the fuck is going on Damian? First Mase, now Ants," I cursed.

Before he could answer, Deano came out with the paramedics and Anthony on a stretcher.

"He's got a faint pulse they said," he shouted with barrels of hope.

Damian and I ran over to them.

"C'mon Ants, don't do this," said Damian quietly.

"He's gonna be cool. Anthony is so smart, he'd probably mend himself," added Deano, trying to share the hope he was feeling.

I didn't know what to say. All moral thinking had been replaced with logic. This was too odd to be a coincidence, but I was glad that Anthony was still showing signs of life.

"Ey, you lot go with him to the hospital. I'm going home, then I'm going round to Tina's to let her know what's going on. Phone me as soon as you get any updates," I said getting into my car.

They nodded and I sped off down the road, trying not to let doubt consume me. He was going to be alright. I knew it.

★★★★★

I got home and paced straight to the kitchen. I needed a drink or two. Pouring out a glass of brandy, I walked to my bedroom and saw the pouch of stones sitting in the middle of the bed.

"I know I didn't leave them there," I said to myself.

I put down my glass and emptied the pouch in my hand. The green stone was missing.

"I don't understand why things are going missing in my own house," I said, irritated.

I disliked being confused about things. No matter how little they may seem. It made you seem like you were going mad. I remembered that I was drunk the night before, so it could be anywhere and I wouldn't even know. I couldn't remember much more than that after leaving the funeral. I thought nothing of it and threw the pouch down on the table. I sat on the edge of my bed, drinking glass after glass. I couldn't stop thinking about Mason and Anthony. Things didn't come together properly. Ever since the robbery – besides drinking and partying all the time, my gym taking off again and my recognition of my feelings for Tina – we've had more complications than anything else. My phone rang and it was Tina. I quickly put down my glass and started getting ready to head out and pick her up, before realising I'd had more drinks than I could remember. I couldn't drive in that sort of shape, even though I felt perfectly fine. I decided to answer her call and switch up the plan.

"How would you feel about coming to mine instead? I came home and I've been drinking. You wouldn't believe the day I've had," I sighed.

"I didn't really want to come out, but I suppose a little fresh air won't hurt. Fill me in when I get there," she said swiftly before hanging up.

★★★★★

An hour later, she turned up on my doorstep waving a bottle of wine.

"Nice to see you too," she said, acknowledging my dejected facial expression.

After making ourselves comfortable in front of a good film, she turned to me. "So, tell me what's made your day so rubbish then?" she asked.

"I found Anthony unconscious at his house today. He's down at the hospital with Damian and Deano now and he's still holding on, but that's not the point. We just lost Mase, now something's wrong with Anthony. It all seems funny to me."

"Oh my God, I hope he's okay. But you can't look at things like that, Foss. Why would you even suspect foul play? No one has anything against any of you," she probed subtly.

I knew she could read the tension in my body language

and wanted me to open up to her. That was something special in a woman; when not only their eyes, but also their heart welcomes you. What would she think of me if I told her I was a thief? Because that's what I was and I was starting to think it had something to do with all the events that had followed the robbery. I knew if I wanted to pursue anything with Tina, I had to be honest from the beginning.

"A few months ago, Deano suggested that we all rob an abandoned house that he heard could make us some decent money. We had all come into hard times and we thought it would be cool, but what we found inside were a load of drugs and money. I was angry that he got us involved in something that risky, but he swore that he didn't know and we just got lucky. We split it between the seven of us and now Mason's dead and Anthony's in hospital. I think someone wants their merchandise back," I confided, hesitantly.

A long silence echoed. It was a few moments before she took it all in. I couldn't blame her because it was a lot to take in. "Foss, Mason's death was an accident and I'd prefer to continue thinking that. You were even there. Anthony is going to be fine once they work out what's wrong with him and do what they have to do. As for the robbery, I can't say I agree with it, but it's already happened now. You have to put it behind you or what was the point of it in the first place?"

She was right, but I knew I was right too. Fair enough I may have been looking into things too hard because of what happened to Anthony, but it didn't make sense to me.

"Stop feeling guilty. I'm not trying to say what you did was right, but it was an abandoned house. It makes it easier to deal with because nobody lives there," she said, rubbing my shoulder.

"Was it really abandoned though?" I asked in a sceptical tone. "Who would leave all of that behind if it wasn't a trap house, Tina? Drugs and money like that is sure hard to come by, so I'm sure the owners will be out looking for the culprits."

"And don't you think it would have happened by now, Foss? Look how long ago it was and you're still here. So are Deano, Rylo, Damian and Justin. Not to forget Anthony is hanging in there too," she replied.

She had a point and her point made me feel like I needed to let it go. We put it aside for the night and I tried to relax. While Tina gave me a massage, I attempted to call Rylo and Justin to let them know what was going on, but I still got no answer. Knowing them, they'd copped off with some girls and were ignoring my calls purposely. My immense comfort eased me into a well appreciated sleep before my phone rang. Frightening my nerves, I jumped up, waking Tina in the process.

"What's the problem?" she asked.

"It's Damian," I said, excited for some good news. I was convinced it was good news. "What's good D? How is he doing?" I asked.

All of a sudden, the prolonged silence caused my convinced tone to fade as I anticipated what he was now going to say.

"It's not good, Foss. He's been getting that skin treatment over the last few weeks and it's caused him to contract septicaemia," he replied.

"What's that then?"

"It's a type of blood poisoning. Apparently his body had a bad reaction to the chemicals or something like that. Don't really understand all that doctor jargon," he replied.

I noticed Damian was talking a lot but not saying much.

"D, is Anthony alright?" I asked firmly.

"No Foss, he's dead – a couple of hours ago. He got worse through the night and yeah, I don't need to spell it out, do I?" he replied softly.

I could hear him welling up.

"I'm gonna phone you back," I said, hanging up.

I walked to the kitchen and poured myself a large drink.

"Foss, what are you doing?" Tina shouted, grabbing the glass.

"Anthony's hanging on, yeah? Well guess what, he's dead now," I replied, snatching back my glass.

"I'm so sorry. I didn't know it was that bad," she answered sympathetically. "What did Damian say?"

"Anthony contracted blood poisoning from the chemical skin treatment he's been getting. And who's the one that encouraged him to go? Me!" I said, gulping down my drink and pouring another.

"Why did he want to have it done in the first place? He was fine the way he was," she sighed.

"Well he didn't think so. He was jealous of us. We always made fun of his appearance but it was only banter. Then one night he told me he basically envied us because of how we looked and how much women we had the potential to get. I told him that if it's what he wanted to do then he should go for it and look where he is now, T," I replied, riddled with guilt.

I broke down, but turned away hastily when I became aware of what I was doing.

"It's okay to cry, you know. And it's even better to do it when you have a shoulder to cry on," she said gently.

She held me as I stopped fighting it. I was a man but I wasn't good at losing people, especially not like this.

Chapter Five

I didn't know it was possible to feel numb in a hot shower. With my brown skin shrivelled and my heart barely beating again, I acknowledged that I'd lost two friends in the short space of two weeks and it was breaking me. The brave face and stunning smile wasn't who I was anymore. I emerged from the water, dripping with confusion – confusion as to why this was happening to me? The worse thing to happen to me *is* actually happening to me. Losing loved ones and no one could provide me with a decent explanation as to why? I called Deano as I got dressed to let him and the others know that we needed to talk and we needed to talk *today*. He knew what it was about; I think they all did. A knock was at the door soon after and they all entered in silence.

"We found out about Anthony this morning. I didn't have my phone on me and even if I did, I wouldn't have been able to hear it," Rylo managed to croak.

No one responded. I went into the kitchen and grabbed us a bottle of drink and some glasses. I had a feeling we would need some Dutch courage to get through this discussion.

"So, I guess I'm gonna be the one to kick this off then?" I said, pouring the drinks.

"Kick what off?" queried Justin.

All of a sudden, Deano grabbed a glass and downed his drink in one go. "I've thought about things in depth and I believe someone or a group, however you want to put it, are targeting us because of the robbery," he blurted out.

It was as if he had read my mind.

"Why are you still dwelling on that, Deano? We went over this and you were the one telling Foss to let it go," replied Damian in annoyance.

"Where have you been for the last two weeks, D? Mason's dead, Anthony's dead and we have no idea what the fuck is going on. Who's gonna be next? It seems like we're just going around in circles," said Deano.

"No, this is bullshit!" shouted Rylo, standing up. "You're the one that brought us in on your little job and now you want to tell us people want their shit back and are willing to kill for it," he added, before reaching for another drink.

We could all see his genuine rage at what Deano was trying to insinuate and we couldn't blame him. At that point in time, Deano was something else.

"Oi, let's remain calm. We're just talking. At the end of the day, it's best to get all thoughts on the matter out in the open because what's been going on lately isn't a game anymore," I intervened, trying to contain the situation.

"No Foss, you can see it in his face that he knew this was dodgy from the start. What aren't you telling us?" continued Rylo.

Normally Deano is quick to defend himself against false accusations, but this time he said nothing. I looked at him trying to stop the thoughts I was thinking, but I had to ask.

"Deans, did you know this wasn't a straightforward job?"

He looked at me in silence before dropping his head in

shame. "I knew there was drugs and money in the house. That night I brought it up when we were on our way home from Mason's, I saw a woman standing outside my house on the phone earlier in the day. She was talking about it as I walked past, but I had no intention of taking any action until you guys brought up your financial issues," he confessed, riddled with guilt.

Before he could explain himself, Rylo lunged over the sofa and his fist connected with Deano's face. Hastily Damian and Justin restrained him, while I stood over Deano on the floor.

"How could you lie about something like this and make us think we were in the clear? How crooked can you get, Deano? To betray your closest friends – the same guys who are willing to ride with you whatever the circumstance. We shouldn't even be mad, more like disappointed," I said, monotone.

That's all I felt: disappointment. I couldn't bear the sight of him at that moment, but my heart said otherwise. Deano may be a crook but when it came to us, loyalty was everything in his eyes. The puzzle wasn't fitting together, so I couldn't feel the right emotions for the scenario.

"The opportunity was so convenient. She didn't notice me and I sure made it out like I didn't notice her. I didn't even get a good look at her face – it was that swift of a moment. When you said you had trouble with the gym, I thought who better to take up the opportunity with than my guys," he explained, desperately trying to get his feeble point across.

"Let's just all sit down and have a drink," shouted Damian over the chaos. "Now, if we're gonna talk about things, we have to do it properly or someone's gonna die tonight."

As much as we wanted to resist, we all agreed that a calm

and collective approach was the best way. There was so much to take in. Emotions were running high and in order for everyone to leave here in one piece, I contained my irritation and sat back down solemnly.

"I admit I agree with the prick. Someone probably is after us, but that still doesn't explain why Mason and Anthony died the way they did. I mean, we were right there when Mason collapsed. Who could have got to him at the club without us noticing?" I said, quickly becoming bewildered all over again.

"They were nothing more than accidents, that's why Foss. If someone wanted to take us out, they would need to know who we were and what we do on a regular and I can't see that happening, can you?" replied Justin, convinced we were blowing things out of proportion.

"Anyone could if they really put their mind to it. We done exactly what we needed to do when we decided to rob the house and I know if I'd lost that amount of money in cash and drugs, I'd be out with a vengeance too," replied Deano arrogantly.

"Right now, you need to keep your mouth shut. Your input is irrelevant. You didn't even see the woman's face so we have somewhere to start. You're useless," said Rylo, surprisingly calm.

"Okay, think about it logically," continued Deano, completely ignoring Rylo's imperative. "Killing us in a common way would raise too much suspicion. We don't know who they are, so they could have easily spiked Mason's drink without us noticing and caught up with Anthony at the clinic once Foss left him," he formulated.

No one said anything for a moment, realising it was the most paramount explanation we had so far, even if it did come from the Judas of the group.

"Let's stop this now because it's gone far beyond the little joke we're making it out to be. How are we meant to move on and grieve if you're constantly going to bring this up?" asked Justin, highlighting that he'd had enough.

Even though Deano was making the most sense he'd ever made, I couldn't see someone going through all that trouble.

"Listen, I'm sorry I got us into whatever mess we're in and I don't blame you if you all were to cut me off right now, but I had good intentions and nothing less," pleaded Deano.

Despite the betrayal we were all feeling at that moment, I still saw Deano as one of my guys. He made a mistake and he's going to need to earn our trust back, but we needed to stick together right now. If someone was pursuing us, then we had to think fast.

"It's too risky for us to fall out now, but I highly doubt anything is going to happen to us. Deano's feeling guilty and therefore being irrational about things. Foss doesn't know what to believe, but I know that their deaths were accidents and that's how it's going to stay for me. I'm going home," said Justin, before walking out crudely.

It was clear to see that he was hurting the most and didn't want to keep going over the same thing, but something was telling me this wasn't right.

"I think you all should go. Everyone's got shit to think about, so we'll link up when we link up," I said, clearing the table.

Rylo didn't waste any time and was gone before you knew it. I think being in the presence of Deano was grating on him from the moment he told us he knew this was a dodgy deal. He was zero tolerance when it came to any form of disrespect as it gave him the opportunity to hit something. Deano was a traitor even if we forgave him for his deception, but he would be useful at that time to bear the brunt of the consequences. As I closed the door, I wondered what that discussion had proved. Damian, Justin and Rylo were convinced that it was Mason and Anthony's time to go; Deano was nothing but scum to me at that point in time and I knew if my mind kept doing overtime like this, insanity would take over.

★★★★★

Throwing myself into work was the way I dealt with all the trepidation. Working my fingers to the bone in what I called the graft to happiness always made me feel good. All this nonsense with Deano and the robbery was affecting my ability to live normally. Justin phoned me as I was unwinding over some paperwork.

"What are you doing tonight? It's time to get back out there; strengthen the team again," he said, upbeat.

"Is Deano going?" I asked hesitantly. I wasn't ready to forgive and I certainly wasn't going to forget what he did.

"I haven't asked him yet, but I was planning to. Foss, I understand he's a snake in the grass, but we've been through too much as a unit for it to end like this," he proclaimed.

I think, out of all of us, Justin was the most defensive against cutting Deano off.

"I didn't say he was going to be a problem because I'm sure he knows where he stands with me already, but it's Rylo you need to be convincing. What did you have planned?" I replied.

"There is a party in Central. Some girls I know got me on the guest list with three friends of my choice, so what do you say?"

"I've already made plans to spend the night with T, so I'll have to give it a miss. Have you asked Damian?" I asked.

"Ah, you know how Damian is – can never be bothered to do anything that involves travel. Its cool, Rylo said he's coming, but I just thought we needed to address the tension. The way we are doesn't feel right," he added.

"We're cool Justin, but things need to die down. The wound is still fresh. Anger is more than aggressive at the moment and no one has time for the drama. You're welcome to come link me if the party isn't to your liking," I invited.

Justin had too much heart at times. He could understand Deano in a way that none of us could. The way his mind worked and why he did certain things. I made my way home, enjoying the thought of a night in with a princess. When I was with her, it was like all the other issues weighing me down disappeared. Her intelligence was stimulating; sitting down looking in her dark brown eyes, she made me eager to expand my own knowledge while I fed hers. When I felt stressed, she had that magic touch that set me adrift in peace. Even though we weren't official, the effect she had on me was. What was 'official' anyway? A concept devised by man. I knew she was mine and she knew I was hers – well, I hoped she did. It was still early days, but I was sure things would blossom into something bright. On my way home, I stopped off and picked Tina up. As I pulled up, she was already standing outside waiting.

"Why don't you answer your phone?" I asked as she got in the car.

"I'm not always there when you call, but I'm always on time," she sang smiling.

"Fair enough, serenity," I laughed.

"So how was your day? I haven't seen or heard from you in a while, so fill me in," she queried.

I loved the way she always took an interest in me and what I did.

"It was a good, productive day. And it'll be even better once we crack open a bottle and you fill me in on your day," I said as we entered the house. A hard day's work was exactly what I needed to put my demons at bay. I found working so therapeutic because I always had something going through my head.

"I've finally sorted out the club. We're going to sell it and put half the money towards charity organisations that help people with drink and drug abuse," she explained gently.

You could tell it was a sensitive subject but she was willing to do this in the memory of her brother. I thought it was a brilliant gesture.

"Can I tell you something?" I requested randomly.

"Well, you're going to anyway, so go ahead."

"You're more beautiful than you give yourself credit for. And I'm not just talking about your bright eyes and exceptional smile. You have a big heart and your aura expresses it so much. It's the most attractive element about you. Even when you're hurting, you're still thinking about others," I said honestly.

"Why thank you," she said, grinning. "You make me laugh. I'm someone who believes that laughter is the core of most things. An argument can fizzle out if you manage to make your other half laugh. A depressing day can be uplifted with an amusing fact. Laughter is the resolution to many things," she said, softly.

"I've never thought about it like that, but I agree that

laughter is a meaningful concept. I think I'm a deep person but I do avoid focusing on any one emotion too deeply. I can be a bit cocky at times, but I've earned my bragging rights and that's how I sleep at night," I replied.

"I think it's good to have an open mind. I wouldn't say you're cocky but you can let your pride get the best of you at times. I would describe you more as driven to be the best at what you do."

"I must agree with you on that too. My pride can definitely be my weakness but it's just a trait embedded in me, I suppose. As time goes by and I recognise my mistakes, I'm sure I'll get better," I replied, genuinely believing my words.

The kind of discussions we shared were spontaneous, yet so interesting. The topic would indirectly change into a sudden, continuous flow of conversation that never became boring. She grew on me more and more with the more time we spent together. Over a bottle of Rosé, we created good vibes and good times. Most importantly, I was considering letting my guard down for the first time in a long time. It was time to embrace something special.

★★★★★

I was awoken by a series of continuous loud bangs on my front door. Tina and I had fallen asleep awkwardly on the sofa and my neck was killing me. As I tried to make sense of all the noise, I noticed it was 4am. I immediately became enraged, realising the lack of respect someone had for me at that time in the morning, but as I got closer I heard Justin calling out for me.

"Foss, wake up! Foss!" he shouted, circling hysterically.

"Justin, calm down! Tell me what's going on," I said, baffled.

"It's Rylo. He got into an argument at the party tonight and the guys came back down for him after he left without me," he spluttered hastily.

"Let's go then. Who are they? Where are they from?" I said, rushing to get my trainers on.

"No Foss, they've got to him already. Just come now!" he urged as he ran to my car.

"Foss, what's the matter?" said Tina croakily.

"I have something to sort out quickly. I'll be back in a moment," I said, closing the door behind me.

I was puzzled to the point where my hands were shaking. Anxiety replaced my fatigue as I drove, taking Justin's muddled directions. He was rambling on so fast that I couldn't make out his words quickly enough.

"Alright, calm the fuck down!" I bellowed as I slammed on the brakes. I couldn't make out anything that was going on and it was distressing. Before I went any further, I needed some clarity.

"Justin, talk to me. Take a deep breath and just talk," I said, gripping his head in my palms.

"We went to the party and he left before me. I left soon after and found him battered in the road. Take the next corner and park up," he pointed, swiftly changing the subject.

Trying to maintain a calm mentality at this frenzied time, I continued to drive up to the house party, which had now turned into a crime scene. Police scrambled from guest to guest trying to recreate what had happened. Ambulances raced past, skidding to a halt. It was chaos.

"Where is he? Is he in the crowd somewhere? How bad is

he hurt, Justin? It looks like a riot broke out," I shouted over the deafening crowds.

I turned around and couldn't see Justin anymore. I'd had enough of trying to piece together this joke. It was early morning and I was on the road for what? I had all the company I needed back at home and I'd ran out on her. I wouldn't be surprised if I went back and she was gone. Hindered with frustration, I broke through to the centre of the madness and finally found Rylo – mangled. I heaved and turned away sharply. All I could repeat in my mind was 'look at what they've done to him'. I attempted to get closer as I repressed my urge to vomit, but was dragged back by a police officer.

"Get off me! That's my boy! That's my boy!" I shouted as tears soaked my face.

Justin re-emerged and took over my restraint. I now understood why he was talking so much and saying so little. He knew if he had told me this had happened before we got here, things would have been different.

"Justin, who did this?" I asked, panting.

He stared back at me teary-eyed and said nothing.

"Who, Justin? Who!" I shouted again. I couldn't take it all in.

"Foss, let's go back to yours and I'll tell you everything I know. Things are hectic out here and there's nothing more we can do. We have to go," he replied, steadily pulling me away.

What I saw wasn't a dream. The sight of a twisted frame, once a delicate skeleton, was traumatising enough. Knowing that the twisted frame that lay before me was Rylo made it wrenching.

★★★★★

I stormed into the house wondering how this could have happened. We were being hunted and there was no doubt about that, but by whom? How did they know where to find us and how were they pulling this off so easily?

"Sit down and talk to me, Foss. You look like you're going mad," said Tina, trying to reassure me.

It was too late for that now.

"Justin, what the fuck happened out there?" I said with my fists firmly clenched.

My breathing symbolised the intense red emotion running through my body. Flashes of his body threatened my psychological ability to stop myself from being sick. I couldn't keep still but then again, I couldn't move.

"We went to the party and was chilling at first…" he began.

"Get to the point, Justin!" I forced.

"He got into an argument with a woman when she didn't want him to buy her a drink. You know how Rylo is, if you give him any reason to kick off he would. Some guy stepped in as I was walking over to see what was going on. They got into their own argument and Rylo spat in his face and walked off. I followed after him and he said that he was cool, but he was going home. He didn't want me to go with him, so I went over to the same guy he'd just been arguing with and told him to let it go. He nodded, walked off and that seemed the end of it," he explained, slightly trembling.

You could tell he didn't want to miss out anything significant.

"So, what happened when you left the party?" I asked. Although devastating, I found the tale intriguing.

"I had this uneasy feeling about the whole situation. The guy was moving funny; always on the phone looking at me and shit like that. I left about twenty minutes after noticing I couldn't see him anymore. When I turned the corner on Milly Avenue, I saw a group of men running down the road. My first instinct was to run them down to see what was going on, so I did for a few metres. It was then that I recognised Rylo on the floor and stopped. He was torn up, Foss."

Tears rolled down his face as he reached the pinnacle of his story. Tina lay numb in my arms, taking in every word but with no reaction. As for myself, I didn't know what to feel, think or say. Everything around me felt stationary. All I heard was the voice of Justin talking as I sat in a trance. His tone of hurt and devastation was just enough to let me know that I was still in reality, still there.

"He was alive when I knelt down beside him. He was trying to tell me something, grabbing my shirt. It sounded like 'ouse' or 'louse', but I couldn't make out anything else. Maybe it's the name of one of the guys that jumped him, I don't know, but he was in bad shape and I knew he wasn't going to make it, as bad as it may seem. I lay his head on my jacket and tried to keep him talking. After I called the ambulance, a crowd started to gather around and I ran off. I couldn't have people thinking that I'd done that to him. That's when I came here and got you," he concluded.

It was a struggle to listen, but I'm glad I knew the ins and outs.

"Did you catch any of their faces as they were running off? There might be a slim chance of finding them," I queried, feeling deflated.

"It was too dark to make out faces, but I know there were seven of them. That's the least of our problems, Foss. You were right all along. Someone is targeting us and, right about now, they have the upper hand – first Mase, then Ants and now Rylo. We're three men down with nothing to go on and I'm failing to see how we're going to get out of this one," he said, sighing hopelessly.

"I'm leaving," said Tina, intercepting sharply. "I'm not going to sit here and listen to anymore of this shit. You know how I feel about Mason's death and you're persistent with this theory that he was murdered. You lot got yourself into whatever joke this is meant to be and I'm not involved," she continued as she grabbed her things.

"Please T, don't go. We don't know what this is ourselves. We're just throwing out some scenarios trying to establish the truth," I said, tugging her shirt gently.

"Let go of my clothes, Foss. All this deception, acting like you're decent when you're really not. Look at what has spiralled from your stupidity: extreme paranoia and stress. I don't want anything to do with it and I don't want anything to do with you neither, none of you," she pointed, before slamming the door behind her.

What more could go wrong for one individual in one night? Tina and I were starting to make progress. We'd both been through a lot and that's what we had in common. That's what drew us together. Now she was gone due to our own mess. The worst thing is that I let her leave because it dawned on me that this was serious. There was no way I could let her become affected by any of this, but on the other hand, I didn't want to lose her. I cast my mind back to my immediate priority, which was Rylo.

"What are we going to do? Tina isn't the issue right now, so forget about her. We need to work this out now and properly," Justin said sternly.

"If it is someone, how would they know that you were at the party? And how would they know Rylo and this particular guy would have an argument? Nothing fits together and it's frustrating. How did they know Anthony was getting skin treatment to even find him at the clinic? How did they know Mason would be working at the club on that specific night? They clearly have some serious tabs on us to get this close without any of us noticing," I pondered heavily.

"I can't understand any of it neither, but maybe this is all a ploy. I mean, targeting us in a common way as Deano suggested would raise too much suspicion. No one would guess that someone killed Mason because he was drinking all night and taking cocaine. It would be an easy opportunity to spike his drink and trigger his seizure," he analysed profoundly.

"That could be possible, but what about Anthony? He died of septicaemia, which is an infection. How would they be able to carry that out? They would have to have some medical background or knowledge," I asked, getting drawn further into the discussion.

"That is what I'm still trying to figure out. Septicaemia is an infection so maybe at it's purest it can be injected and have the same effect as if he were to contract it as a side effect of his treatment. No one would have thought anything of it," he said.

We were putting the puzzle together, but still had no idea whether we were on the right track. Even so, we were grateful that we had somewhere to start.

"Rylo was in the right place for whoever it is after us to set him up. It must have been a set-up. They see that he's had an argument and tension is mounting, so they use that as a diversion to disguise what they really were trying to do. When he left, they probably followed and carried out their deed, leaving everyone to assume the same guy from the party is the same guy that attacked him," he said, digging deeper.

8am was creeping up on us and we were straining to keep the thinking going. We didn't know what our next step was going to be and at the same time, we didn't know what was coming next.

★★★★★

Justin and I made our way to Deano's house, calling Damian on the way to meet us there. We hadn't slept a wink and it was time to get things in the open before they found out what had happened from anyone else. Driving down what seemed like endless stretches of road, my state of mind was nothing more than turmoil. Justin was the same as we drove in silence.

"What are you doing here at this time in the morning?" Deano asked, yawning.

Justin and I stepped past him without a word.

"Oi! What are you lot doing? You can't come walking in my house ignoring me. It's eight in the morning on a Sunday," he cursed.

"Rylo is dead, Deano. Damian is on his way and I haven't slept all night, so ease up on the shouting and sit down," I said, rubbing my temples vigorously.

"What do you mean Rylo's dead? Is this some dumb joke because I knew about the drugs and the money? It's not funny and if it's like that, then you lot need to get out," he replied angrily.

"Do I look like I'm joking? Do you really think I would

be here out of all the places on earth if I was joking? You don't want me to come over there, so please, please refrain from speaking anymore," I replied, looking up sharply.

His facial expression altered from anger to anguish.

'What happened? When…?" he said, trailing into disbelief.

No one said anything. He didn't even deserve a response. Finding out that he was responsible for every downturn we've had since the robbery made me harbour nothing but resentment for him and his greed. That was the fundamental aspect of this matter. Deano's greed had got the best of him once again, yet *we* were all sharing the permanent consequences. It was then that Damian turned up, just in time for the explosion to come.

"What's all this about now? I thought we were going to let things blow over with Deano, then talk in a calm manner when we were all ready. Look at the time you have me out of my house," he cursed with minor fury.

Damian always had a problem with being asked to do anything, so we took his rant on the chin. We had much bigger things to deal with.

"Rylo was beaten up last night after the party he and Justin went to. We're here because he's dead and it's Deano's fault," I said sternly.

"Hey, slow the fuck down, Foss! What do you mean he got beaten up and he's dead? How?" he said, seriously.

"Why the fuck have you both asked me what do I mean Rylo is dead? Am I not talking English? Do I have to spell it out in blood for you to understand what I'm saying? Rylo is gone and we know it has something to do with the robbery and that's where Deano comes in. This shit is too bizarre to be a coincidence, so it's up to Deano to figure out how to get us out of the same mess he dropped us in," I stressed emphatically.

We sat in dumbness as Deano and Damian began the same process that Justin and I had endured the night before. Wondering how it had happened and trying to piece together an incomplete puzzle.

"So, are you going to tell us more or leave us in the dark?" asked Deano, submissively.

"You should be left in the dark because you brought the dark upon us," replied Damian.

"Long story short, he got into an argument with a woman at the party and a guy stepped in to cool it down. Rylo then began to argue with him, before spitting in his face and leaving without me. I left soon after and found him in the road. Seven guys were running away, literally leaving him for dead," Justin explained briefly.

You could see that even recalling the night brought tears to his eyes. There was another long pause before anyone was willing to say anything. I was tired and things were moving too slow for my liking.

"This is what I'm saying: Rylo's death is the last straw for me. We need to do something and we need to do it now. I'm not going to lose my life over bullshit I should have never been involved in. I accept that it was my decision to get involved in the first place, but if Deano hadn't held back on the facts, my decision would have been different and final," I sighed irritably.

"Did you see any of their faces, Justin?" asked Deano with a burst of energy.

"No, it was dark. Why?"

"Why? Because we're going out there to touch someone,

that's why. If the guy at the party had some involvement in Rylo's killing, he must know something about who may be after us – it will at least be a good starting point," he replied.

I honestly believe that suggestion was the smartest way Deano had ever used his logic in his entire life.

"So, what are you proposing?" asked Damian.

"Justin may not have seen the faces of the men running away but he saw the face of the one in the party. I say we find out who he is and where he is to find out what's going on. I feel guilty as it is and if another one of us gets caught up in this, I won't be able to contain myself anymore," he replied firmly.

"That actually sounds like a legitimate first step, but how is that benefitting us? We still committed burglary. If we start going around breaking members of the public, I'm sure it's going to backfire on us," said Damian, making perfect sense.

"Yeah, I don't think that's the answer neither. Plus I've seen too much blood recently and it's messing with my health now," said Justin, cracking a slight smile.

"So what's the answer, Justin?" I asked sarcastically.

"Are we meant to wait until they come to us? Well fuck that, because I'm not feeling that at all. We have to nip this shit in the bud now," added Deano.

"I agree with Deano," I said simply. "We find the guy and talk to him. If push comes to shove, then we do what we have to do."

There were only four of us left. In the shortest space of time, I'd lost three of my best friends and didn't know how to cope with such a combination.

"Well, it is what it is. We need to get some sleep, regroup tomorrow and get this over and done with because shit just got real," finalised Deano.

CHAPTER SIX

When the guys and I met up the next day, the feeling of emptiness surrounded us. Things were so different. The team I had once spoken so highly about had fragmented into nothing more than corruption and resentment.

"Did you find out where the guy from the party is staying from your female friend?" I asked Justin. He always had his sources when it was necessary which, as one beneficial aspect of his lustful ways, had helped us more than a few times.

"Yeah, we spoke last night and she said his name is Xavier and he's staying at the Stallion Hotel on Colin Road. He isn't from these parts, but has been down here for a while to her knowledge. We're just going to talk to him, right?" he asked wearily.

"That's the plan," said Damian.

None of us wanted this to become more than it was, but we wanted answers before more bodies started to fall.

"Justin, you need to relax. We're doing this to save our lives. It's not another petty personal gain plan. It's a matter of survival. Do you understand how serious this is?" emphasised Deano.

"You shouldn't even be here. You're the reason we have to be doing this in the first place. You have no right to say anything about games because you're the biggest player in the room," said Justin defensively.

To all of us, it appeared that he'd been waiting to get that off his chest for a long time. Usually he was the one sticking up for Deano when he got on our bad side, but it was more than evident that he'd had enough just like the rest of us.

"What's the damn point of me being here then? I mean, you all don't want my input on anything. You don't want anything to do with me as a matter of fact. Justin is right, why am I here?" replied Deano, defeated.

"No one is going anywhere. If we don't get this done now, we don't know how long we'll have to even hold grudges. Deano stays and we do this properly," I said firmly. "Now, we're going to the Stallion and we're going to wait outside until we see Xavier go in or out. Then we talk to him, get the information we need and take things from there."

"What do we need to know though? We have so many unanswered questions, Foss, that I wouldn't even know where to begin. And what if he doesn't talk? How are we meant to handle that scenario? This is more than the four of us going to beat up a 'nobody'," said an overwhelmed Damian.

"Can we all just compose ourselves, please? We'll cross that bridge when we get to it. There haven't been any better suggestions, so let's get this done and dusted," I said, walking out of the door.

This was our only lead to finding out what had been happening and how we could put it right. I wasn't willing to let it slip away that easily.

★★★★★

Justin was able to point Xavier out to us as he made his way into the hotel. We had been waiting outside for hours and couldn't afford to miss this opportunity of catching up with him.

"I'm gonna go up to the reception just behind him and act as if I'm a friend and he's gone ahead of me. They should give me the spare key to his room and that's when you guys go in the lift with him and see what floor he gets off at. I'll phone you once I've got the key card and you let me know where to come and meet you. Actually Deano and Damian take the lift, Justin take the stairs – so he doesn't suspect anything," I explained quickly as we crossed the road.

I wasn't sure at the time if it was going to work, but it was the best I could come up with in that short space of time. I walked into the hotel and up to the reception desk in the smartest manner possible.

"I'm sorry for the inconvenience but my friend just came in and has gone in the shower, leaving me locked out. Would it be possible to get the spare room key and I'll return it when we come back down?" I asked carefully.

"What's his name and room number?" replied the receptionist.

As soon as she asked that question, I felt like I had just gone ahead with an impossible plan, until a sudden idea sprung to mind. I text Deano to tell me the room number and pretended to have a hard time remembering, making up a short story about just recently checking in. When he text me back, it was a breeze.

"His name is Xavier and his room number is sixty-four," I said confidently.

"One moment please."

She then handed the spare room key over to me and to my surprise, that was it. My act had been that convincing, I'd got away with it in less than five minutes. No questions or suspicions – nothing. I called Deano to find out which floor the room was on and paced up the stairs as fast as I could. Out of breath, I saw Justin waiting for me.

"What took you so long? He's gone into his room," he whispered.

"I got the room key, so now we just have to get in and catch him off guard. Where are Deano and Damian?" I asked, ready to get moving.

"They're walking around on the floor waiting for us. Let's go," he said, walking out of the stairwell.

Out of all of us, Justin was most affected by the whole thing. He wanted to get back to normal life as soon as possible. We all did. Everything then became a blur. We all regrouped and made our way down to room sixty-four. We were all nervous, but none of us wanted to admit it.

"We have to catch him off guard and sit him down on a chair. We talk to him calmly and then we leave. No funny business because we've got enough going on, do you lot understand?" explained Damian.

He looked more serious than we'd ever seen him and that's when I knew what we were about to do was really happening. We all silently agreed as the adrenaline began to kick in. We didn't know what to expect when we walked in or how he would react at first. We were going into this fully blind and it was a scary moment. I pushed the key in the door and it opened. Slightly pushing it further, I was able to hear the shower running and that he wasn't in the bedroom. We swiftly took up the opportunity to get into position, and then we waited. It was less than fifteen minutes before he came out of the bathroom wrapped in a towel and we pounced. Damian and Justin jumped out from behind the door and restrained him.

"What the fuck is going on?" he shouted, struggling frantically.

None of us spoke and we proceeded to get him seated. Deano pulled up a chair, while Justin and Damian dragged and seated him. As all this was happening, I stood watching the corridor for any unexpected surprises.

"Listen, I don't know what this is about, but I'm not involved," he protested.

Deano pulled out some rope and tied Xavier's hands and feet together so he couldn't go anywhere. I sat on the bed directly in front of him and stared in his eyes. I wanted to break him for what he did to Rylo. The image of his body wouldn't leave me alone. It tormented me every time I closed my eyes.

"There's really no point shouting because no one really cares. We just want to know what you know," said Deano.

"You break into my hotel room and tell me you want to know what I know. How am I really meant to fucking respond to that?" said Xavier cheekily.

He glanced at Justin and suddenly paused.

"It's you," he sighed as he retrieved the memories from that night. "Now I know what this is all about. Your friend got beaten to a pulp and you think it was me." He grinned.

I tried to stay calm. We had one goal and one goal only. I wasn't going to let him wind me up.

"All we want to know is who's coming for us?" I said bluntly.

"What do you mean who's coming for you? What does that have to do with anything? Listen, the game is up and I think it's about time you get out before I call security," he laughed.

Again I kept my cool, but Deano couldn't do it anymore. Xavier was taking this for a joke. As if we had the time to find him and make up stories for no reason. Before anyone could say anything, Deano swung for Xavier's face.

"He said 'Who the fuck is coming for us?' And furthermore, why are they coming for us?" he repeated harshly.

Xavier responded by spitting his bloody saliva in Deano's face, which enraged me. I couldn't cope with the disrespect the peasant was dishing out anymore. We came here with leniency in our intentions. I lunged at him and let my anger take over. I repeatedly pounded at his face with no feeling of remorse. Rylo's body was all I could visualise at that moment and it kept me going. The guys rushed over to intervene and even as they pulled me away, I still couldn't contain myself.

"You kill our friend, you know what we want to know and you're fucking us about," I shouted kicking as Justin and Damian dragged me to one side.

"Calm the fuck down! We got this!" said Damian, in a weird but reassuring way.

"How can you stand there looking at his smug face and not want to kill him? He's mocking us, laughing in our faces. I can't deal with that," I said, hysterical.

"Alright, we understand that shit is real messed up right now. Wait in the corridor and take a few deep breaths. Trust me, we got this," he replied.

I walked out and sat down next to the door. I had so much anger in my heart and it was excruciating. Never have I felt so bitter. My life was unravelling at such a fast pace that I couldn't keep a firm grip anymore. I was so used to being in control that when I wasn't, I didn't know where to turn or what to do. The thought of knowing that Xavier possibly knew what had been going on and had tried to humiliate us at our greatest point of turmoil – I'd had enough of the bullshit. I'd had enough of life.

*****

I found myself walking to the bar at the other end of the hotel. I didn't know what was happening in that hotel room and I didn't want to know. As I sat down drinking glass after glass, I wished I could just walk back to the happiness I had felt before getting sucked up in this vacuum. Even though the gym was failing at least I could still smile once in a while. Each drink was a renewed joy to my soul. Just as I was getting to where I wanted to be, Deano called me.

"Where are you? Xavier doesn't know anything, so let's get out of here," he said calmly.

"What do you mean he doesn't know anything? He must know something. What happened to Rylo then? Why have we lost three of our guys with no explanation? I'm coming up to you now," I replied furiously.

He wasn't getting away with it, acting like he had no idea what was going on when he was one of the last people to see Rylo alive. When I got back to the room, all the guys looked worn out. Xavier was battered and still tied to the chair. I gripped my head firmly upon recognition that we'd just dug a deeper hole for ourselves.

"I thought the purpose of getting me out of the room was

to ensure it didn't go this far," I said, joining Deano on the bed.

"Foss, we tried everything to get this guy to talk and he still hasn't given us anything. There's no way he would take such a beating and still keep quiet. He doesn't know anything, so I think we should call it a day," he replied.

"Call it a day? Deano, look at him. If he really doesn't know anything, you've just beaten him so bad he's sure to want revenge," I sighed.

"I won't seek revenge, I promise. Let me go now, please. This is what I've been trying to tell you from the beginning. I don't know anything about your friend's death," interrupted Xavier. "We argued and that was it. Obviously I was annoyed, but I'm not petty. I didn't even leave when he left. I was in the bathroom doing a few lines before I returned to the bar," he spluttered.

"Now we can add assault to our growing list of criminal activity," I expressed angrily.

"You hit him first and you want to talk about assault. This wasn't the fucking idea you proposed when we were walking in here," Deano replied aggressively.

"Everyone shut up!" shouted Damian, trying to maintain harmony. "We're not gonna get anywhere if we start tearing each other apart. Especially showing this piece of crap when we're not at our best. The bottom line is Xavier has nothing to do with what we're looking for, so let's go back to the drawing board and work this out again."

Stunned by his sudden leadership, we all complied and began to untie Xavier's hands and feet before throwing him on the bed.

"As you've just experienced, we've found you once and we

can find you again. Keep this between us and we won't have any further problems. Is that clear?" Deano warned.

"Loud and clear," replied Xavier weakly.

We walked out feeling less than our worth.

"That was a waste of our damn time and effort," Deano sighed.

Every time he spoke, I contemplated why I hadn't strangled him yet. Why I hadn't watched the life drain from his face for doing this to us – us of all people. As we got back in the car and made our way to my house, I felt sick to my stomach. Our only lead had turned out to be no lead at all. I could feel every precise heartbeat as my blood bubbled under my skin.

"Would it be the right time to asked what we're gonna do next? I mean this has got us nowhere and believe it or not, I'm beginning to fear the things that await us – whatever they are," said Justin carefully.

"Nothing awaits us okay!" I answered strictly. "We're to get back on it and find a solution. Four heads are better than one and together no one can fuck with us. Tonight, you all stay at mine in case our silly mistake at the hotel comes back to haunt us."

I didn't want Deano staying in my house, but I had to put my personal emotions aside if I was going to think straight and get the most out of the night.

"Sounds good to me but we need to remain strong as a unit. We can't have anymore repeats of what happened in the room at the Stallion or we might as well give up now," said Damian.

★★★★★

As we settled down in my living room, I couldn't think about anything other than Tina. At first I thought she had a valid point for not wanting anything else to do with me, but after I kept going over it in my head, I believed she should have understood what I was going through. We'd finally begun opening up to each other and I had thought she understood me.

"You lot make yourself at home. I have to go see Tina and straighten things out," I said. I couldn't hold it in any longer. I wanted to know what this was really about. I didn't know whether it was because she was scared of commitment or just plain scared of me.

"Foss, this isn't the time to be trying to resolve your domestics. We have bigger fish to fry," said Damian.

"I understand, but this isn't just a domestic to me and you lot know that. I have to let her know what's good and if she's still not willing to be with me, then I'll let it go. You lot also know that I believe no woman is worth the chase," I replied in deep denial.

To keep up appearances, I lied to myself knowing that Tina was not only worth the chase, but something to be cherished when caught.

"I hear what you're saying, so go. But we need to sort out our own little problem, so watch your time management," he replied.

"Don't worry, I'll keep it short and sweet. No popping bottles until I get back," I said sarcastically.

I knew what they were like. In times of distress, we all turned to the bottle. I probably would have been an alcoholic if I didn't have the gym to run and a reputation to maintain. That all seemed to be in the past as I made my way to Tina's.

The reputation I boasted so highly about only a few months ago was near enough in tatters and the gym I had built with my blood, sweat and tears was now the gym I had helped to destroy. I let my confidence influence my decision to get involved in something I knew nothing about and now I was paying the price. My stupidity pushed away the one woman that had actually meant something to me since my mother died and all I could feel inside was regret.

As I pulled up outside Tina's house, I sat in the car momentarily thinking of what to say. We had ended on such a harsh note that I didn't want to burn the rest of the bridge we still may have shared. I got myself together and knocked on the door, before waiting nervously.

"Who is it?" she shouted from behind the door.

"It's Foss," I replied, hoping she'd still let me in.

"Go away, Foss. I made my feelings clear and I don't want to go over this again," she replied sternly.

"Hear me out first. I thought you of all people would be here for me right now and all you're doing is making things worse."

"So you came all the way here to blame me for your fuck-up? This just gets better and better, doesn't it? Well, at least I've seen your true colours before I made any stupid decisions. I would appreciate it if you left now," she replied, filled with sarcasm.

"Tina, I'm sorry. I didn't mean it in that way. I'm sorry about everything that's happened and I don't want us to fall out like this," I pleaded.

Sorry was a word I had always found hard to say for two reasons. Firstly, I believed people didn't deserve a 'sorry', regardless of the circumstance, because it had no effect. It didn't change anything. Secondly, I was used to being right all the time and when I was wrong, I was still right in my eyes. I felt it was the time to abolish those morals that had consumed me for as long as I could remember and fight for what I wanted.

"Foss, I can't deal with this, whatever this is. You mean a lot to me, but from what I've heard about the situation, the outcome doesn't look great. I can't afford to get attached to you, only to lose you. I'm the one that's sorry. Go home, Foss. Forget what we had," she replied.

I could hear that she was crying and knew there was no point trying. Imagining her tears running down her caramel skin, I wished I was on the other side of the door to wipe them away. She'd made her feelings clearer than clear and I walked back to my car with a blank perspective on life. It had dawned on me that pursuing someone that didn't want to be pursued was like doing a bench press with no arms: impossible.

I was in a world of my own. I couldn't help but think this was all happening for a reason. All the dirty dealings I had had to do to become comfortable were finally coming back to bite.

★★★★★

"I thought I said don't start drinking before I got back," I said as I entered the house to see the lads borderline tipsy.

"You were gone for ages. Did you really expect us to wait for you?" laughed Justin rhetorically.

I couldn't argue with that. I had been talking to Tina through a door for God's sake. Her words felt like a dent in my character. She hit all the vulnerable areas that I'd spent years hiding.

"So what happened between you and Tina then? Considering what we've been through today, you looked much better before you left," asked Deano.

"Don't ask me anything. I still find it hard to even look at you after what you've caused, so don't think alcohol is going to change anything between us," I replied boldly.

"I know the alcohol isn't changing anything, but the only thing holding us together right now is this mess and I've said my apologies. What more do you want, Foss? Blood?" replied Deano.

"You're the reason why everything with me and Tina has gone poof! Vanished! She doesn't want anything to do with any of us, especially me, because we're making Mason's death harder for her to deal with," I shouted as I stormed into the kitchen and poured myself a drink.

"What the fuck did I tell you lot about the arguments? It's like you can't help yourselves when this is the time we need to be looking at the bigger picture," preached Damian. "If this is how things are going to continue, then we're as good as dead. Now, both of you sit down and calm down. Even if that means having a little wank to relax yourself – I'm at my wits' end with you two now."

Damian was the oldest out of all of us and it was evident that he was the problem-solver when it came to tension arising in the group. He had a valid point, but the way I felt about potentially losing everything made me so angry when I looked at Deano. As things got worse, my hatred for him deepened.

"It's hard to be civil with you after what you did, but I guess I'm willing to make a damn good effort for us as a unit. Not for you, for the *unit*," I clearly emphasised.

"Foss, I can't express how bad I've been feeling since this

all started, but I'm trying to make amends, put things right and stay as a unit. Not for me or for you, but for all of us – including Mason, Anthony and Rylo," replied Deano genuinely.

For the first time, I saw real remorse in his eyes. I felt that if he could swap all he had gained to make this end, then he would have. That was something I'd never felt before when it came to Deano.

"Thank God you've finally called a truce. Now we can leave the strategy planning until tomorrow and unwind over this bottle," sighed Damian with great relief.

"I say we play a little game," suggested Justin. "We take a shot and reveal something about ourselves from the past. Something significant and something we don't already know. The more shots that are taken, the deeper the discussion. Hopefully it eases the atmosphere and makes us realise why we became friends in the first place. I'll start," he continued.

At first, we all thought the game was stupid. We honestly believed we knew everything we needed to know about each other, but considering the state we were in, we engaged in the process of getting to know each other for a second time. Justin took his shot and began.

"My parents died in a car accident while we were on our way to a camping site one summer. I was only fifteen. I found it hard having to move from care home to care home. I couldn't establish any routine and just thought my life was over. But it was like my prayers were answered when I started developing feelings for one of my carers at seventeen. It wasn't the feeling of attraction but more of affection. She reminded me of my mother so much. Once I was old enough to live on my own, the relationship between us changed and it was like our bond had broken. She stopped contacting me and I partly believe it was because she was developing feelings for me that she believed to be inappropriate. Since then, love hasn't been in my vocabulary, especially for women. I get attracted, get what I want, then on to the next one," he said calmly.

It was a dark note to begin with, but it gave us a direction to go in. Instead of bombarding him with questions on why he was only telling us this now, we continued and Damian went next.

"When I was made redundant, I turned to alcohol as you all know and that's when my life really took a turn for the worst. Rena and I would argue everyday until one night, when I was drunk out of my skull, I hit her. And I didn't just hit her once. I kept hitting her until her features were no longer visible anymore. That's when she left me and took baby Milly-Anne with her. I refused to get a job because I was convinced the world was against me. I managed to get over my drink addiction, but after all the attention surrounding the assault and the custody battle, there was no chance of me finding decent work again. Now, I'm this twenty-seven-year-old bum. Still young, but with no aspirations."

It hit us hard to know we'd been friends for the longest time and he'd never really spoken about why he and his wife had gone their separate ways. We had always tried to stay out of things we believed didn't concern us, but you would think he'd have told us something as serious as that. The atmosphere had frozen as we took in everything that was said, without saying a word. It was Deano's turn next and I was intrigued by what he had to say.

"Well, you already know my mum was a drug addict. Heroin was her best friend – but I think the person who sits here before you today evolved from the abuse my father inflicted on me while my mum was knocked out. I remember when I was nine. He'd just come home from work and my mum had passed out in the bathroom with the door locked. He came into my room and touched me, even kissed me on my hands and neck. I'm sure you can guess the rest. It carried on until I was thirteen. That was when I'd had enough and turned to crime just to keep me out of the house. Every time I was arrested, I felt nothing but relief knowing that I'd be spending a night in a jail cell – able to get a decent sleep without having to look over my shoulder. By the time I was seventeen, my only option was to run. I became the thief I am today and as I got better and better at what I did, greed got the best of me and became all I knew," he concluded, before taking another drink.

A round of deep sighs circulated the room as the lads geared up for my story. They already knew I had had a rough start to life, but I'd never told them the gory details. It's not something you want to keep going over when it's hard enough to deal with silently. I took my shot and took a deep breath.

"You all know about my brother Ryan being jailed for killing my stepdad, but I never told you how it escalated to that point. It all started when Winston came home drunk one night and he got into an argument with my mum. Things were just about to get violent when Ryan came home. At the time, I was so happy to see him. It was as if he'd come to the rescue. He told me to go upstairs and lock myself in my room. Sitting behind my door, I could hear Ryan and Winston fighting and breaking things all over the house. After a few minutes, I went out to the top of the stairs and saw Ryan standing over Winston. There was so much blood. My mum had ran out the house to God knows where and all I could see was blood. I ran down the stairs and took the knife from Ryan and told him to run. He'd stabbed Winston twenty-three times. If that wasn't rage at it's hottest, I don't know what is. I called the ambulance and waited. It was the longest fifteen minutes of my life, sitting there looking at a massacre. When the police finally caught up with him and he went on trial, he was charged with manslaughter. Despite my statement about it being self-defence, the jury had a different theory," I explained.

"Why haven't you gone to see him?" asked Damian.

"Ryan has got into so much trouble since he's been locked up that I doubt I'll ever see him again. Since then, my ego has made me. I realised I didn't want to end up where he was and that I could do anything I put my mind to. I mean, the graft it took to get out of the poverty my mum had left me in wasn't easy – so when I achieved what everyone believed was impossible, my pride just continued to elevate. My mum and I lost contact and a couple years later, I found out that she had committed suicide. I couldn't blame her. Our own family failed to intervene when they should have and let the situation turn into what it did. Damn I miss her," I concluded.

"A drunken tongue really is an honest one. That discussion was more than revealing," said Damian, trying to break the ice.

"It was, but also hard to listen to at some points. I think I speak for all of us that our little game done the job. I feel like we're how we were before all the craziness started," said Justin slowly.

Each of us slipped into a thoughtful state of mind as we tried not to cross any boundaries in relation to what we'd spoken about. You didn't really know which questions might touch a nerve. After the meaningless banter to disguise our true emotions, we drifted off into our own, previously discarded, memories.

Chapter Seven

I was awoken by the clinking of glasses in my kitchen.

"Who's in there?" I croaked in the dark.

"It's Justin. I'm having a drink because I can't get back to sleep," he said as he came to sit back down.

Damian had gone to lie down in my bedroom, while Deano had made a bed on the floor. I looked at my watch and noticed we'd only been sleeping for just over a couple hours and it was still early in the morning.

"Why did you wake up in the first place?" I asked. I thought I'd help myself to a drink to put my mind back to rest too.

"Nothing in particular, but when I fully woke up, all I could think about is what we'd spoken about earlier. It was some really deep stuff," sighed Justin.

"Yeah it was. Damian really had it rough, but I can't justify the fact that he beat his wife in that way. The same way I can't justify the fact that Winston thought it was okay to do the same to my mum – but Damian has made some serious progress to be as calm as he is now after everything he's been through," I said as I went over his words again in my head.

"Yeah, I really felt bad for him, you know. But it's Deano's story that makes me think more than anything else. I always thought I knew him inside out, but now I understand why he is the way he is. He didn't have anything and now when he has the opportunity, he'll take anything. I actually feel sympathetic towards his greed," he said, finishing his drink.

I did the same and made myself comfortable again. I had a burning question to put to Justin, but I feared touching a nerve. I did so anyway and hoped for the best.

"Why didn't you tell us that the death of your mother was the reason you never want to commit to women?" I asked as I lay staring at the ceiling.

He shuffled into the same position and sighed, "I didn't think I needed to at first. It didn't seem like a major deal to me until I actually sat down and thought about it. I'd always hated thinking about it though. To think about how they died and how my carer just faded away. But it feels good to get it off my chest since I haven't told many people."

"I understand why you wouldn't want to talk about it and I think I speak for all three of us that we feel good you could share that with us," I replied.

"It was about time. You lot finally know why I am the way I am with women. Sex is the priority and pretty much the only goal. I'm not willing to love someone when they're just gonna be taken away from me, you know what I mean?" he said.

"I hear you loud and clear. You're not ready to take that step yet, but in time you will. Just don't let your lustful ways get you into any trouble," I joked.

"Maybe, maybe not," he said, before rolling over.

As I did the same, I couldn't help but wonder why he didn't ask me about my story – but then again, I was glad he didn't.

*****

The next time I opened my eyes, I saw Deano and Justin having a laugh.

"Finally awake, sleeping beauty?" asked Justin sarcastically.

"What do you mean *finally*? What time is it?" I asked.

"Just gone eleven. What's the plan for today, boys?" Justin said as he rubbed his hands together.

"Do we really have to talk about this now? Damian isn't even up yet," Deano sighed.

"Talk about what? The fact that we've still got to think of a way to get out the mess you dropped us in? Yeah, maybe we should wait until Damian is up. Why don't you go get him?" I sighed with great annoyance.

"You know what, I will. Let's just get this over and done with so we can get back to normal," he said, heading to my bedroom.

I wasn't up to arguing. It was best to decide what had to be done, so we could put all of the trouble behind us.

"Foss!" Deano suddenly shouted.

I ran to the room with Justin right behind me.

"What's the problem?" Justin asked, panting heavily.

"Damian isn't waking up. I don't know what's wrong," said Deano, letting us through.

"D! Damian!" I shouted as I checked his pulse. My facial expression said it all.

"He's dead, isn't he?" said Justin, holding his head in frustration.

"No, he can't be! How? Who could have got in with us all here? No Foss, check again," urged Deano in denial.

"He's dead, Deano!" I shouted as I walked back into the living room.

With my fists clenched, the hot tears rolled down my face as the thought I'd been trying to erase from my mind came to light. There wasn't anyone after us. It was something more than that. We were being punished, punished for our sins. I didn't know how it worked, but I knew it was the work of something supernatural – something beyond our control.

"Foss, what are we going to do?" said Deano, failing to fight back his tears.

"Phone the ambulance," I replied bluntly.

"What then? Foss, we're dropping like flies with no explanation," said Justin angrily.

"Call the ambulance," I repeated calmly.

They took the hint that I didn't want to say anything more with Damian's body laying next door. It wasn't long before the ambulance came to collect Damian and we had to deal with the police.

"All three of you need to put on something more appropriate and come down to make a statement about what happened," said the officer.

"Why do we have to go down to the station as if we're suspects? Damian was a brother to us," said Justin.

"Okay, we can do it here if it makes you feel more comfortable. Were you all here all night?" he asked, proceeding with his routine questions.

"Yes, we had a small drinking session before we went to sleep for the night," I replied, strongly disinterested.

"Okay, so what happened?" the officer continued.

"We went to sleep and Damian was fine. We woke up first and had a little chat in here for a while before Deano went to wake Damian up. You know what happened from there," I said hastily.

I wanted to get them all out of my house so I could get my mind right.

"Okay, is there anything else you would like to add? I understand this is a hard time for you all, but the more information we have, the more chance we have of finding out what happened as soon as possible," the officer concluded.

"Listen, if I could tell you anything more I would, but I can't. We need time to come to terms with what has happened," I replied, exhausted.

"Fair enough, Mr Franklin. We'll be in touch soon," the officer finalised.

Soon after, everyone began to leave and the house slowly became empty. The three of us sat staring into space, refusing to face the music.

"Foss, how could this happen? We've been here all night," emphasised Justin in disbelief.

"You still don't understand!" I shouted. "No one came here during the night and no one has been coming for us full stop. This is karma, Justin. A force is punishing us for robbing that house and I think our only option now is to return whatever we have left of that dirty money and hope we can rectify our wrong. Think about it, we had a few weeks of the high life and ever since we've just been surrounded with death and destruction," I explained.

"I'm not returning anything. What makes you think you're right about this? That's all I have and returning the money would only mean we've gone through all of this for nothing," said Deano defensively.

"You got any fucking better ideas, Deano, because I'm all ears," yelled Justin in frustration. "This is a small price to pay for the rest of our lives and if Foss thinks that returning what we have left is the only way to fix your fuck-up, then we're doing it."

Justin's reaction surprised the speech out of Deano. It seemed as things got worse, we saw an angrier side to Justin. His words made us recognise that returning to the abandoned house was our only solution if we wanted to keep the rest of the mind we had left.

"We'll do it then. When and how are we going to carry this out?" sighed Deano, seeping devastation.

"We need a bit of time to get the money together and get in and out as soon as possible. In case anything should go wrong, we should bring some weaponry. We still don't know what it is exactly that we're up against, so we need to be fully prepared," I explained carefully.

"I say we do it tomorrow. I can get my share of the money together today and I'm sure Deano can as well – anything to end this once and for all," said Justin, throwing back some shots.

"Alright, tomorrow it is. Deano, are you paying close attention? Because if you mess this up again, it won't be just karma you're trying to avoid," I said firmly.

"I hear you Foss, but you don't have to speak to me like that. I understand the situation and I'm willing to give up all the money I have to put this right."

The next day wasn't a walk in the park. I couldn't sleep, constantly wondering if I was next. I didn't want to leave the house, but then I realised we weren't safe anywhere. Damian had been sleeping in my own bed when he had died. Even after going over it multiple times in my head, I still couldn't come to terms with him being gone. I still couldn't come to terms with all the losses I had endured, including Tina. I didn't even get the chance to ask him if he was okay after he revealed to us what he did. Deano and Justin were on their way over with the money and we were finally going to be free. The thought alone made me feel that tiny bit more relieved, but sitting down looking at the money I had to return made me feel like I was going to have to start from scratch. Then again, I believed it was all worth it.

"How are you feeling?" asked Justin.

"Considering the circumstances, I've had better days," I replied as we changed into suitable attire for break-in number two.

"You know what he means, Foss. We're all feeling the same feeling – fear," added Deano.

"I'm not fearful, I'm ready. There's a difference. I understand what you're saying, but I think talking isn't the best thing for us to do right now. We have enough doubts as it is," I explained.

We had already come to the conclusion that whatever was going on was no human act. We didn't know what we were going to encounter when we went back to that house, but fear was nowhere in sight for me. Numbness was all that remained, alongside my mounting confidence in getting my life back.

★★★★★

As we drove to the abandoned house, I had the same uneasy feeling I had had when we went there for the first time – only this time, there was a valid reason. What were we going to find? And was returning what we stole really going to save us? Whatever the outcome, it was worth a try. We all had nothing left to lose. The car came to a stop and we all looked at each other.

"We go in the same way we did before and leave the money in the exact place we found it," I said sharply.

"Understood," they replied simultaneously.

We ran up to the door we had previously smashed and entered the house. A heavy smell of something rotting caught my nostrils.

"For fuck sake, I could have sworn this wasn't here the first time," Deano squealed.

"Keep your voice down and hold your breath," replied Justin.

We tried our best to remain quiet, but after a while the smell was overpowering.

"Give me the money," said Deano when he found the spot.

"Are you sure this is where we got it from? Everything has to be right Deano," I emphasised.

"It was definitely here. I remember you were over by the bookcase and I called you over here. Everything we have left is here, so let's go before this putrid smell stays with us permanently," he replied in annoyance.

"Even though it's not everything we took, it still shows we have heart returning what we have left, right? Good always prevails over evil, right?" said Justin, searching for some reassurance.

As we fled down the road, a different atmosphere filled the car. It felt as if we'd been let go by something. I felt positive and the uneasy feeling I had had was now gone. They always said that the brain was a powerful tool. I could have felt that way because I felt like we had done what we needed to do – made our wrong right – but then again, it wasn't confirmed that we had changed anything at all.

"What do you think this means for us now?" asked Justin calmly.

"I don't know, but let's hope the only way is up from here," I replied as we sat in the car outside Deano's house.

"I think this calls for a drink, don't you?" suggested Deano.

"You think anything calls for a drink," laughed Justin.

"Go on then, I suppose a few won't hurt," I added, making myself comfortable in his freshly furnished house.

Deano pulled out a bottle of well matured whisky from his kitchen cupboard.

"Damn, Deans. Where did you get this beauty?" I said, admiring the bottle.

"An old friend gave it to me after I did him a favour. I guess there's no better occasion than celebrating the start of our lives again," he replied, sliding over some glasses.

"Trust me when I say I'm going to be on the straight and narrow from now on. Not that I was off track in the first place, but everything that has happened has made me see things in a better perspective," said Justin, sipping his drink.

"I understand what you mean and I feel the same way. At the end of the day, the gym is my pride and joy, but not worth my life. Working hard to get what I want is the priority. No more short cuts," I replied.

"I think this was meant to happen. Not saying that it was ideal the way it did happen, but we needed this wake-up call to show us that our lifestyles needed to change. At the rate I was going before everything got on top of us, I'm surprised I haven't had an STI," laughed Justin. "But maybe settling down is what I need now. No more promiscuous movements. I guess I just need time to respect myself, find myself again."

"I can't say I disagree with that, but after what you've been through, it does shine more light on the reasons as to why you became so detached from your emotions the way you did," I replied.

"I know, but it's time to let go. I'm not getting any younger and after losing Mase, Ants, Rylo and Damian, I need all the support I can get," he said.

"You and me both. Tina means so much to me and this situation has tarnished everything we had. I don't blame her. We reminded her about Mason's death every time she was around, but what can I say lads? I miss her like mad," I expressed.

"Foss, I can't remember the last time you've felt like this about a woman. If this really is all over then, now is the best opportunity to get your woman back for good. I can put my hand on my heart and say out of all the men in the world, Mason wouldn't approve of anyone being with his sister more than you," replied Justin.

"I hear you, but you know how I am. Committing to someone is a big issue for me. I made myself to be work-orientated so I didn't have to deal with the emotional side of life, but I can honestly say she has changed that mindset," I said, genuinely.

"Your best bet is to go for it," Deano added. "You win some and you lose some, Foss. If rejection is on the table, then at least you know you can actually feel emotion towards someone now and hopefully move on with your new mindset," he said.

"Hopefully. How are you feeling about things?" I asked Deano.

It was the first time I felt fine talking to him. I didn't have the boiling sensation inside me to throttle him anymore. I was starting to feel better and better as time went by.

"I know I need to change my view of things. I put you lot at risk and I'm the underlying reason why we've lost four of our closest friends. That alone will torture me for life, but a good start to easing my conscience is to get out of this crime game and never look back," replied Deano, downing his drink swiftly.

"To be real with you Deano, it will take me a long time to get over what you did, but you're one of us and sitting here together after everything that has happened shows that forgiveness is the only way to start the healing process. From now on, we have to vow that anything we do has some sort of good intention behind it. I believe that's what we were meant to learn from this experience. It was a message telling us that the way we were acting, we would have ended up like our friends anyway. Now we've got a second chance and we have to make the most of it," I explained.

"I'll definitely drink to that," said Deano raising a toast.

★★★★★

My head was spinning after hours of boozing. Justin and Deano had fallen asleep, but I took my drunken state as an opportunity to expose all my inner feelings to Tina in one last push to make her see that I feel she is the one for me. It was late, but I knew it wouldn't happen how I wanted to if I were sober. I would hold too much back, so I decided to call her and let out what I needed to.

"Hey T," I greeted, partially slurring.

"Foss, are you drunk?" she immediately asked.

"Not drunk, maybe a bit tipsy, but forget about that. I want to talk about you," I replied.

"Look at the time. What have you been doing?" she asked, sounding concerned.

"Nothing, just listen."

"Okay, I'm listening," she replied, sounding sceptical.

"I know things haven't gone as smoothly as we've wanted it to, but I can't let you go like this. Not after the way you've made me feel. Not after the way you've made me realise I can feel again. The lads and I were involved in something beyond our control, but it's over now. I'm sorry you had to hear all the things we did due to our paranoia," I said openly.

My heart was literally on my sleeve.

"So this 'thing' you had to deal with, how come all of a sudden you're not involved? You were certain that foul play had a role in Mason's death and repeatedly reminded me about it like grieving wasn't hard enough."

"And as I said Tina, I'm sorry for the negativity I've caused you. It is all too much to explain, but what you should know is that we have dealt with it. We saw the error of our ways and that's how we made things right," I explained.

"Foss, you mean a lot to me. Even though we've had so much distance between us lately, I think about you every day – but when you became obsessed with your little theory, it made me remember why I can't be with someone. I will always be placed on the back burner when something else comes along, instead of us communicating and dealing with the matter together. I'm done, Foss. I would love it if we could stay friends, maybe go for a drink sometime," she replied, trying to sugar-coat the rejection.

"No Tina, I refuse to *just go for a drink sometime* with you. I have never in my days felt like this about someone and it's about time I say what I have to say so you understand. I want you by my side so we can build a world around us. I want to invest my time in you, which is more than I'll do for any other woman. And this is all coming from a heart that's grown as big as space in the last few months because I've learnt what it's like to feel pain again, but also love."

I found it amazing how alcohol can make such a strong man so weak. A long pause took over and I began to doubt my revelation.

"Can I come over?" she asked calmly.

"Of course you can, but it's late and I don't want you walking the streets at this time just to see me."

"I'll take a cab down. See you in a bit," she said, hanging up suddenly.

I was confused. I didn't understand her reaction and why she suddenly wanted to come over. After I'd just let out what I thought I never could, was she coming here to stick the knife in even more? Tell me how much I'm no good and possibly retract her feeble friendship offer? Sometimes the drink doesn't do the justice you want it to. I woke Deano and Justin up and they made their way home. It was about twenty minutes later when I heard a faint knock at the door.

Stumbling to the door I shouted, "Who is it?"

"It's me. Who else would it be?" she replied sarcastically.

When I opened the door, she stood with her arms folded, silently looking into my eyes. She then held my face and kissed me passionately. Shivers ran down my spine as I could feel the love she secretly had for me. I picked her up and brought her inside. I lay her down on my bed and looked at her.

"What is this all about?" I asked.

"The last thing you said to me, 'a heart as big as big as space'. Who says that?" she smiled sweetly.

“Well, I was saying what was on my mind at the time and I meant it,” I replied.

“I know you did. And I want you to know I mean it when I say, I got you if you got me Mr Franklin.”

She pulled me in closer and kissed me again. I knew this was it. I knew this was my moment for life.

★★★★★

I woke up to a face I wouldn’t mind waking up to every morning. I smiled slightly as I watched Tina sleep peacefully. As I got out of bed to make some breakfast, I glanced at the black pouch on my side table as I walked to the kitchen. At first I couldn’t remember what it was, but when I went over and picked it up, I heard the stones. The pouch felt lighter than usual, but then again I didn’t pay much attention to it in the first place. I emptied the stones in my hand and only three fell out. I knew there had been seven when I’d first counted them, but all that remained was violet, yellow and blue. Feeling in a mood of bliss at the fact that Tina and I were finally official, when I heard her wake up I put the stones back in the pouch and didn’t give them a second thought.

“Good morning,” she said, sitting up.

Her beautiful figure wrapped tightly in my white bed sheets made her something to admire.

“Morning T. How are you feeling today?” I asked as I sat on the bed next to her.

“I’m feeling great. What about you?” she smiled.

“I feel good. I was just about to make some breakfast. Do you want anything?” I asked.

“Yes please, chef. Some pancakes would be nice. Only if you can make them though,” she joked.

“Real men can cook and clean too, you know. Who do you think keeps this house in check?” I laughed. I didn’t want to ruin the moment but I wanted to know what she was really feeling about last night. “You don’t regret coming over do you? I asked.

She crawled over to me and wrapped her arms around me as I sat with my back to her. “I don’t regret one second of it. Last night was the best time I’ve had in a while and it was with you. I’ve brushed everything in the past under the carpet. You make me feel special. Why would I walk away from that?” she said, kissing my shoulder.

“I know, but I just wanted to make sure. You are special and you should feel that way all the time. I’m going to make you feel that way all the time,” I replied.

She kissed me again on my forehead and lay back down.

“I’m gonna get these pancakes started, then we’ll have a lazy day,” I smiled as I rubbed her head gently and made my way to the kitchen.

I intended to cherish every minute spent with her from this day forward.

CHAPTER EIGHT

Life was blissful. I had the woman of my dreams, my business was thriving and I was planning to expand. I was in a good place and everyone could see it in my face. There was only one pit hole in my road to happiness, which was my friendship with Justin and Deano. It had been a while since we'd seen each other as we tried to get back into normal life. After the funerals had been held for Anthony, Rylo and Damian, we all went our separate ways to focus on other things. Most of all, it helped me come to terms with what I had lost and hold onto what I had gained. Tina and I had just returned from a lengthy holiday in Mexico and we were both feeling refreshed to have enjoyed a change of scenery.

"Foss, I've been thinking and I think you should get in touch with Justin and Deano," she suggested randomly as she unpacked her case. "It's been months since you've spoken to them properly and I think you could do with a little guy time after being stuck with me for three weeks."

"Why do you say that? I personally think the space and time apart has been good for us," I replied.

"Yeah, maybe so, but it would still be nice to see how they've been getting on,"

"They could have got in contact with me but they've chosen not to, so I'm sure they're fine T," I replied.

"Stop being stubborn and invite them over for a drink. I'm not saying you need to become best buddies again if you don't want to, but I'm going to visit Mum this evening and I thought they could come over and you can have a little catch up."

I saw her point but I was choosing to ignore it. It was too soon for me. We went to hell and back and I needed time to put it all behind me properly before I could maintain a proper friendship with Justin and Deano again. I'd been in great shape for the last few months and I didn't want to ruin it making any hasty decisions. I think the minimal contact I'd had with the guys had done just the trick, but to keep the missus happy, I agreed.

"Okay, I'll have them over for a few drinks. I suppose it would be nice to know what they've been getting up to, but I'm not making any promises," I said.

"Good. I'm leaving out at around six o'clock and probably won't be back until tomorrow, so make sure I come back to find you in one piece," she joked.

"I won't be overdoing it after that holiday. Tell Mum I said hi and I'll pick you up tomorrow."

"No, you don't have to do that. I can make my own way back," she replied.

"And please tell me why I'd have my woman walking when I have a perfectly working vehicle?" I asked sarcastically.

"Shut up," she replied, slapping me.

The kind of relationship we had was just right. She was my best friend, my girl and my guidance.

★★★★★

I had called Justin and Deano to come over for a catch up and a couple of drinks, but I still had my doubts. It had been hard after we'd buried the men who were closest to us. It really hit home that all could have been avoided if we'd just made the right decision to pass up Deano's offer like we always did. It still hadn't fully sunk in that it was all God's work, or so we'd assumed – but I'd like to think of it that way. Whatever it was that changed our lives forever had given me hope that on the right path, the outcome would always be for the better. While I sat in front of the TV thinking about the way things were, the doorbell rang.

"Long time, brother," smiled Justin.

"I know man, how have you guys been?" I asked as we made our way inside.

"I've been good. I've got a new job as an accountant, so I'm making some real money now. Had to do a few courses but it was worth it. I feel like I have a purpose now, you know?" replied Justin.

"That's really good to hear. I'm proud of you. How about you Deano, what have you been up to?" I asked.

"I haven't been doing much with myself besides redecorating my house. It held too many memories, both good and bad, so I felt it was time for something different. What about you? And how is the beautiful Tina?" he asked, smirking slightly.

"Oi, keep your eyes off my woman! What's wrong with you?" I laughed. "We've just come back from a well-needed three-week holiday in Mexico. I thought a getaway would do us some good. Now it's back to reality and back to business," I added.

"Well, not for me. I've got a bachelor party to go to in Las

Vegas. The same one I was meant to go to a while back but it got postponed. It will be my last opportunity to lust over some female company," laughed Justin.

"When are you heading out there?" asked Deano.

"Next week Wednesday. I still have to finalise a few things with work, but then I should be set and ready to fly out."

"Sounds like you're planning to have a wild time. Make sure you get back in one piece and without a ring on your finger," I joked.

"He probably won't come back at all," laughed Deano.

I thought it would be difficult, but it felt good catching up with Justin and Deano again. I realised that the spark our group had shared would always be here.

"So, I know it's probably not what you want to hear, but I'm going to ask anyway. How have you been coping with what happened?" Deano asked carefully.

I automatically thought he had asked so as to ease his conscience even more. Knowing that we were feeling okay after what we'd experienced made him feel less guilty and allowed him to forgive himself that little bit more.

"I don't mind talking about it, but I wouldn't say I would bring it up as a topic of conversation. I'm at a stage in life where I'm happy for all the right reasons. After we buried the guys, it was a chapter closed with another ready to open. We were thrown a lifeline and it was just what I needed. How about you Justin?" I asked.

"I've tried my hardest not to even think about it. Just like Foss, after we buried the guys, it was like a new start for me. Instead of wasting my time chasing women, I got the skills I needed and found work. I can't complain about anything right now," he replied.

"It's all about channelling my energy into what I already have, rather than what I desire, that allows me to sleep at night," I said.

Deano remained silent as we discussed our progression.

"What about you, Deans? It was random that you would bring it up but not say much," asked Justin.

"What can I say? Even though much time has passed and we seem to be in the clear, we've still lost Mason, Anthony, Rylo and Damian. And to make it worse, knowing I'm the cause yet I'm still living makes it difficult for me to move forward in the way you two have. I'm just dealing with it in my own way; keeping my mind occupied and staying clear of any trouble," he explained.

"As long as we're moving forward, it doesn't matter how it's happening. Now let's stop all this depressing talk and get this session started," I said, diverting the conversation abruptly.

It was obvious that the guilt currently drowning Deano was becoming too much for him to bear. He seemed isolated in his own mind. Then again, I didn't want everything being brought to the surface again. I wanted to leave the past in the past.

★ ★ ★ ★ ★

I didn't hear when Tina came back in. I thought she was staying with her mum for the night.

"When did you come in?" I asked, rubbing my eyes.

"It's 4pm, Foss. I stayed at Mum's last night and you were meant to pick me up today," she replied.

"Ah T, I'm so sorry. I guess the lads and I got a bit carried away with the drink last night. I can't believe I'm only waking up now," I sighed.

"It's alright but don't make it a habit. You done enough drinking on holiday," she smiled, kissing me on my forehead.

"I'm gonna have a quick shower, then come and join you on the sofa with some popcorn and a good film. You can tell me how Mum's getting on," I said, hugging her around the waist.

"Alright, but you're making the popcorn just for forgetting to pick me up and I'm choosing the film," she laughed.

I stood under the soothing water and allowed my mind to slow down. Having a good time with Justin and Deano was a nice way to round off a restful holiday before getting back to work. The gym had been in safe hands with Ray and Janet investing so much effort into making it what it was while I was gone. Suddenly, I was overwhelmed with sadness as thoughts of Deano crossed my mind. He wasn't himself anymore. When I looked into his eyes, it was like nothing was there anymore. In one way I looked at it as a good thing. He needed to change if he was going to get anywhere in life, but I think the way the lesson was taught weighed heavily on his heart and took a lot more than we thought it would. What he needed to understand was that it had happened and we're here. There was no time to dwell when we still had a life to live. Feeling deflated, I wrapped myself in a towel and went to sit with Tina.

"I know I smell fresh, you don't have to tell me," I said sarcastically.

"I wasn't planning to, but clearly you've lost your clothes," she replied.

"I'm a man. Men should be allowed to walk around naked if they want to."

"That's fine, as long as I'm the only one home and you're walking towards me," she smirked.

"I had a good time last night with Justin and Deano and they've made progress, but I can't help but think Deano needs some professional help," I confided.

"Why do you think that?"

"Justin and I have tried our best to deal with the death of the guys and make the most of what we have, but it's like Deano is just floating around in limbo – as if he's oblivious to how lucky he is that he's still here even though our friends aren't," I explained.

"It's just guilt, Foss. He could have done what he needed to by himself, but chose to involve you all. Now he assumes that their deaths and the robbery are related, when really it's his paranoia. This is something he is always going to have to deal with whether he gets help or not."

It hit me that Tina had no idea that the robbery *was* related to the deaths, but when I realised, I wanted to keep it that way. Some things are best left unsaid, even though what was going on was more that just a *thing*. It freaked me out, so I could only imagine what it would do to her. I'm sure she would run a mile all because I couldn't keep my mouth shut.

"Yeah, that's probably it. I'm gonna keep a close eye on him. He may be trouble, but he's trying to reform and that's good enough for me," I replied.

"That's good. I'm glad you've made amends. I know what the friendship means to you and I don't think you should let it go to waste. There are only three of you now," she said.

As her advice sunk in, the memories of our friendship consumed me. It made me recognise that she was right.

"So, what do you think I should do? Spend more time with them or what?" I asked.

"Personally, I think that's the answer. A trip would be ideal

– maybe a weekend in Germany as a little lad's get-together. I heard it's really nice down there. What do you think?" she suggested.

"That's actually a good idea. It's not too expensive and would be a nice experience, but Justin's going Vegas next week for a bachelor party, so financially he may not be ready for another mini-break."

"Mm, that's true. Put it to them anyway and see what they say. The worst that can happen is they say no and we think of something else," she replied.

"Yeah, I really like the thought. The next time we meet up, I'll let them know and see how they feel about it. Sometimes I wonder what I'd do without you."

"I don't know what you would do neither to be honest," she boasted, "and don't wait until you meet up. Phone them so you have time to sort everything out if the answer is yes."

"Alright, Mum," I joked.

Every time I looked at her, I realised how lucky I was to still be here.

★★★★★

Walking back into work felt like walking into my second home. Even though the smell of people getting fit lingered and I had mountains of paperwork, it was good to be back.

"Where's the vibrant Janet today?" I asked Ray.

"She's round the back. Nice to see you back looking refreshed," he replied as we gestured.

"It's good to be back. How have things been while I've been gone? Everything's looking good, but let me know what the damage is," I enquired. Even though I'd invested most of the money I had gained from the robbery, with all that had occurred, I wasn't sure about anything anymore.

"Things have run much smoother than it did before you left. As you can see, the refurbishment is complete and we've got all our new equipment. The response to our recent promotional methods has been exceptional – and, most importantly, I'm seeing new faces and our old faces are leaving happy," he explained.

"That's what I like to hear. You and Janet have kept on top of things every time I'm absent and I appreciate it more than I can say. And not just as an employee, but as a friend too," I said.

"It's the least I can do. This is our job and you've been good to us. Plus, I think I speak for me and Janet when I say we get great satisfaction out of what we do."

As soon as her name left Ray's lips, Janet appeared from the locker room with her familiar smile beaming.

"Hello, Foss. Good to see you. It's been too long. How have you been? And how was the holiday?" she said, firing questions at me.

"It was very restful. Tina and I had a great time, but now I've got a few tough decisions to make," I replied.

"I see. Well, things have been fine at our end. We've got a few new staff, so when you have the time I can introduce them to you and run through their credentials. So far they are on a two-month trial and after that the decision is yours about who to keep on and who to let go," she explained.

"That sounds like a plan. I want to get through some of this paperwork first, then you can show me what's new around here," I replied, walking to my office.

"Okay. I've got the back room to finish cleaning, so I'll be in there when you need me."

It was a great feeling knowing that I could be a million miles away and my two senior staff manage to keep things under control. I sat down in my dearly missed swivel chair and embraced my surroundings with a grin on my face. As I went through my papers, I tried to imagine how I would feel if I had to let the gym go. It was the only remaining tie I had with the robbery because I'd invested over half of my findings into it – but this was my life, my graft. I knew I wouldn't be able to stand by and watch someone tear down what I had worked so hard to build. It was a thought to be considered, for the complete fresh start I intended to have. I called Justin to ask how he would feel about a mini-break to Germany when he got back from Vegas.

"How are you, Foss?" he answered.

"I'm alive and well. Back at work today, so I'm feeling a bit pumped up. Quick question, when you get back from Vegas, what would you say about another little weekend away to Germany? This time with Deano and me, doing what we used to," I suggested.

"That sounds good to me, but it would have to wait a few weeks after I come back. The amount of money I'll be spending in Vegas will definitely leave me broke until then," he laughed.

"I understand. That's what I was saying to Tina when she brought it up, but we can book for a couple weeks later that shouldn't be a problem. I'm gonna phone Deano and see what he thinks about it, then finish up my work for today. If I don't speak to you before you go away this weekend, then enjoy yourself and get back safe," I said.

"Of course I will. I'll be on a new path when I get back. And I'll bring you back some real liquor. Talk soon," he concluded.

Tensions between Deano and I still existed, but were a lot less strong. After we spoke about what happened at my house, I realised he was hurting more than any of us because he had to face it for the rest of his life. I think that was punishment enough. As the phone rang, I tried to sound as positive as I could.

"Yo Deans, what's going on?"

"Not much, just finishing up some painting. The house is starting to come together now," he replied.

"That's good man, you've been working on it hard. I have a quick question to ask, then I have to get back to work. What do you say about a weekend trip to Germany when Justin gets back from Vegas? Put things behind us for good and become the friendship group we used to be," I said genuinely.

"To be honest with you, I wouldn't mind a nice break to Germany. It would be good to get away for a while. When are you planning the trip for?" he asked.

"It has to be after Justin gets back from Vegas and gets settled down again, but I'll look up the tickets and let you guys know how much it would cost roughly."

"This should be fun," he laughed.

"It will be," I laughed. "Anyway, I have to get back to work so I'll update you," I said before hanging up.

I raced through my paperwork and before I knew it, I had nothing left to do. It had been a productive day, but I wanted to get home to my woman. I loved the way she took an interest in my day at work and fitness in general. Tina made me look forward to the end of the day even more. I packed up my things and headed out onto the gym floor.

"I'll see you tomorrow, Janet. You can run through the new staff with me then, since we didn't get time to do it today. Tell

Ray I would like to see you both after work tomorrow too. I won't keep you too long, it's just for a casual staff meeting," I said.

"Alright Foss, have a good evening and I'll see you tomorrow," she replied.

On my way home, I began my usual thought process. I was twenty-six-years-old and had never considered starting a family. I understood that Tina and I hadn't been together for a long time, but it felt like we had. What if I was Mason or Rylo? They'll never be able to have kids of their own. It was something that would always bother me. Our kids would never play together or have the life we all should have had. Well, that wasn't going to be the case for me. I just hoped Tina felt the same way.

★★★★★

The next morning was bright and I was raring to go. As each day went by, my good mood increased. I didn't know if it was my brain trying to make up for all the sadness I'd felt not long before, but I wasn't complaining. I moved swiftly around the house with a spring in my step as I rustled up a quick breakfast and got myself ready for work. I kissed Tina as she slept and flew out of the front door. The only thing I'd thought about all night was starting a family. I've never felt so strongly about being in a relationship, let alone taking it that step further and thinking about bringing new life into the world. On the other hand, I would completely understand if Tina felt it was too soon, but what was too soon? This experience has taught me that people put boundaries on their lives that don't need to be there. All that matters is what makes you happy. I hoped Tina saw things in the same way and felt committed enough to take this step with me.

I had planned to take her out to dinner and openly talk about it. I assumed a nice meal in a calm setting would be most ideal for the type of conversation I wanted to strike up. Even though I was confident about how she felt about me, I still braced myself for disappointment. My baby desire was also in relation to why I wanted to meet up with Janet and Ray after work. If Tina did feel mutual about starting a family, I would need to take a long-term step back from the gym. There were honestly no other two people better than Janet and Ray to leave in charge while I was gone. I wanted to promote them both, so they could effectively maintain the success of the gym. On my way to work, I was constantly debating with myself about whether it was really what I wanted to do – to leave my gym in the hands of others. It was only when I walked into the busy gym and saw the performance of my team that I knew I would be at peace with the idea.

"How have things been so far?" I asked Janet.

"Same old really. Busy as usual," she smiled.

"I can see that. Remember that after work I would like to see you and Ray. I'm taking you both for a drink. It's the least I can do for all the hard work you guys have been putting in."

"That's really nice of you, Foss, thank you. I'll let Ray know when he comes in from his break," she replied enthusiastically.

"Great, I'll see you both at six."

As the day went on, I couldn't help but admire what I had built from the ground up. Before the robbery and what had followed, my pride would have directed me rather than my heart and I would have never considered leaving my work in favour of working on my personal life. I guessed near death experiences changed things for the better; made you think about living. After a hectic day and a few customer disputes, it was time for me to wind down and think of how to approach the conversation I was planning to have with Ray and Janet. I pulled up outside the entrance of the gym in my car and waited.

"This is a really cool gesture, Foss. Thanks," said Ray as he and Janet got into the car.

"Believe me, you guys deserve more than just a drink. For years you guys have dedicated your time into making sure the gym has the high standards that it does. You pointed out the error of my ways. I should be thanking you," I replied sincerely.

We drove down to a local pub that I saved for special occasions like this. I've always had a close relationship with my employees, but I'd brought Ray and Janet to the pub more than a few times. It gave me the opportunity to see the other side of them when they weren't at work.

"So what's this about then? Is there a problem?" asked Janet.

"No, the gym is perfectly fine. I wanted to talk to you about your positions within the gym,"

"See Ray, I told you we were probably being laid off. That's why we're down at the pub acting as if everything's okay," sighed Janet.

I broke out into laughter. "You thought I was going to fire you? After all the praise I give you both and you thought I was going to fire you? I actually brought you here to offer you each a senior management position in the gym. I need to take a long-term step back from work and would be relieved to know that I have two reliable points of call in charge."

"So you're saying you want Janet and me to be the new senior managers of the gym?" asked Ray as he tried to confirm if he had heard correctly.

"Well, that's only if you choose to accept. It would mean working full-time and a considerable pay rise, but you're not obliged to say yes. If you want to continue in the positions you're already in, then I'm completely happy for you to do so," I clarified.

There was a long pause in which I sipped my beer to avoid awkward eye contact.

"I'm up for it," said Ray.

"Me too. I love working at the gym. It's not just a job to me, but part of my social life. The customers are great and I'm sorry for wrongly assuming you were about to sack us," added Janet.

"Oh its fine, don't worry about it. Does this mean I'm speaking to my new senior managers now?" I asked proudly.

"Yes you are," said Ray as he raised a toast.

"To new beginnings," added Janet.

"To new beginnings," I replied.

★★★★★

Time had gone by quickly and before I knew it I was rushing home to let Tina know we had a dinner date. Women and the time they took to get ready would always be a mystery to me. I arrived home to see her with a bottle of wine snuggled up in front of the TV. She looked comfortable and in some way I didn't want to disturb her, but my urge to get what I needed to say off my chest was much more overpowering.

"Hey love, how was work today?" she asked.

"I'll tell you in the car. Right now you need to make

yourself beyond beautiful because we have a dinner date in approximately an hour's time," I said, rushing around.

"Dinner date? Where? Why are you just telling me now?" she replied confused.

"It's a surprise T, so can you work your magic and meet me in the car when you're done."

I had the quickest shower ever because I needed to go and pick up her gift before we went to the restaurant. I always left things to the last minute and expected everyone else to keep up with me.

"Why have you just come and sprung this on me, Foss? Now I'm stumped for what to wear," Tina moaned as she threw more and more clothes on the bed.

"You'll look gorgeous in anything and you know that."

"So where are you going now then?" she asked.

"I have to go pick something up first and then I'll wait for you outside when I get back. I won't be too long."

"Well I should be ready by the time you get back – now you've finally finished in the bathroom," she smiled.

I swiftly got myself dressed and made my way to see a long-time friend of mine. I had known Karl since I first had the intention of starting my gym. He was a diamond collector and had done me a lot of favours in the past. I'd arranged for him to make me a customised bracelet for Tina and the occasion. It cost me quite a bit but I believed she was worth every penny. Karl gave me a considerable discount that I couldn't complain about so I felt good, but I had a niggling doubt that Tina would take the gesture the wrong way. After bringing up the baby idea and showering her with gifts, I didn't want her to think I was somewhat bribing her. Either way, it was a risk I was willing to take.

"Long time no see," laughed Karl as he let me inside.

"I know, man. With the gym and everything else going on, I don't make much time for a social life anymore."

"I completely understand. We're all trying to make the same living out here, so you don't need to explain. I know you're on a tight schedule right now, so here's the bracelet for the missus. I'm sure she'll appreciate it," he replied respectfully.

I opened the box to see the most beautifully intense ocean blue diamond bracelet. It was stunning. Karl had an amazing talent that I was fascinated by. I knew Tina would love it.

"Karl, you've honestly done me proud once again. Thank you," I said genuinely.

"No problem Foss, anything for a good friend. You've got me through some rough times and I'll never forget that," he said, shaking my hand.

"That's what mates are for. I have to shoot off now, but we'll link up soon and have a proper talk. Thanks again," I replied, before I ran back out to the car.

I couldn't think about anything else but the smile that would light up the room when I gave her the bracelet. Trying to hide my excitement, I beeped twice to let Tina know I was outside. At first I thought that knowing her she would still be getting dressed and I would be sitting out here for much longer than anticipated, but it was a few minutes later that I saw her stroll towards me looking like the definition of elegance. I was lost for words as her appearance seemed to overpower me. She was amazing in all areas and elements.

"How do I look?" she asked self-consciously.

"You look stunning, Tina. Even though I say it to you often enough, you are a striking individual," I expressed.

"Thank you, honey. You're looking suave yourself, but I still don't understand why this was so random. Are you sure everything is okay?" she asked in a sceptical tone.

"Of course everything is okay, why wouldn't it be? I just want to take my woman out for a nice meal and some good conversation," I smirked.

"I think you're up to something. If you've done something Foss, just tell me. Don't sugar-coat the matter with a slap-up meal because you're feeling guilty."

"Listen Tina, nothing is wrong. I promise. All I want to do is take you out and for us to have a good evening. Is that too much to ask?" I replied.

She sighed heavily.

"Now, can you relax and be my date for the night?" I asked as I helped her out of the car.

"Sure. I'm sorry for being a bit touchy, but I just wasn't sure that's all. This is a lovely gesture and I'm very grateful. Thank you," she replied, before kissing me.

We walked into the restaurant and sat at our table. I was beyond nervous. She had already thought I was up to something dodgy, so the night could have gone either way. I suggest having a baby and she's happy about it, or I suggest having a baby and she flips her lid.

"Okay, so now is the time for you to come clean and tell me what brought all this on? You had all day to let me know about this and you left it until the last minute for what reason?"

"I wanted us to have some alone time so I could talk to you about something that's been on my mind a lot recently. I thought a nice atmosphere would make things that little bit better," I explained.

"I see. Well go ahead, I'm all ears love."

I took her hand and looked into her eyes. The thought going through my head at that point was 'How the hell did I become this?' Someone who used to be so detached from their emotions was feeling more emotion than ever.

"We've been together for some time and I know you're the one for me. I haven't felt like this about anyone before and even though I thought commitment was never for me, I'm willing to commit to you. Possibly a little me and you too," I said, slipping the idea in delicately.

My heart was racing to the point where I began to think everyone else could hear it too.

"Are you trying to say you want to have a baby?" she questioned calmly.

I couldn't read what she was thinking, which scared me. I could usually analyse her body language and interpret it, but she was blank. I couldn't work out whether she was keen on the idea or trying to play it cool because we were in public.

"I'm trying to say, I'm ready to have a baby if you are. We're not getting any younger and after I lost my friends, I realised life was too short. I can't think of anyone else more suitable to be a mother to our child," I replied softly.

I had never felt so engaged. As we were speaking about something so deep, it was a moment I didn't want to end – spiritual. I pulled out the jewellery box and slid it over to her.

"This is a little thank you for being there for me. We've had a few ups and a lot of downs, but it's clear we got through it because you got me. I want you to know I got you too, T," I added.

She opened the box and stared at the content before staring back at me.

"Foss, I don't know what to say. It's lovely and must have cost you a fortune, but I can't accept this," she said, handing it back to me.

"Why not? You don't really like it, do you?" I questioned.

"No, it's gorgeous. Honestly I don't think I could have chosen anything better, but I just feel like I don't deserve it. And you don't have to give me these expensive things anyway."

"How can you say you don't deserve it? Most women would run a mile if the man they wanted was constantly paranoid about people being after him. All the things you had to hear because of me and all the tears you've shed all because of me. You deserve more than a bracelet and to be quite frank, you deserve more than me," I replied honestly.

All she did was hold her wrist out for me to put the bracelet on. As I did so, I saw tears roll down her face.

"You're just right for me and don't ever think different," she said quietly.

I had started to think that maybe the restaurant wasn't a good idea, but she changed that.

"And the answer is yes. I would love to start a family with you. Not because of the gifts and endless flattery, but because you have appreciated me more than any man has before. You've given me faith in happiness again," she added as she smiled blissfully.

It was like music to my ears. There was a chance that I was going to be a dad and what made it even better was that it was with the woman of my dreams. As each day went by, I realised more and more that Justin, Deano and me were lucky to still have lives to carry on with.

"You know what, how about we scrap dinner and go home

to start this baby-making process," grinned Tina as she pulled me out of my seat and towards the car.

Looking at her take control of the situation showed me that I wasn't making a mistake and she was really up for the new step we were planning to take.

"Sounds like a good idea to me."

CHAPTER NINE

Both physically and mentally, I was ecstatic. Tina and I were the happiest we'd ever been, with trying for a baby giving us both something to look forward to. Another event on the agenda was our wedding. I acknowledged that I'd done things completely backwards when I'd asked Tina about the baby idea without even proposing marriage. I had already planned to spend the rest of my days with her, but marriage made things more official. We were engaged and eager to tie the knot, but we knew we had other things to focus on. Overlooking the gym would be difficult with all the other plans we had, but I knew Ray and Janet would keep me updated. Everything seemed to be falling into place perfectly. Justin was due back from Vegas today and I couldn't wait for him to tell me all the gory details. I had spoken to him the day before he had left and he was in more than good spirits imagining all the exotic spirits. His flight was meant to be landing at 4pm, so I offered to pick him up after I quickly popped into work. I wanted to see how Ray and Janet were coping with their workload. I called them both into my office for a little review.

"This is just a quick follow-up guys. I won't keep you too long. The bottom line is how are you handling things? I know it might be a bit overwhelming at first, but what are you feeling personally?" I asked.

"Everything is good with me. I'm settling in okay but still need to grasp a few things before I can work out a routine," explained Janet.

"It will happen in due time, don't worry about it. Additional training can be provided if you get stuck. What about you Ray? Getting on alright with your new duties?"

"Yeah, it's more challenging than I first thought but it's a challenge I'm up for. Taking things in my stride until I get the hang of everything."

"I'm glad to hear that because I have some good news. Tina and I are engaged and are trying for a baby. I've only told you two for now and would like to keep it that way if you don't mind, but yes, I am officially a taken man," I smiled.

"Congratulations Foss, I couldn't be happier for you. This all makes sense now. You're going to be away from work much longer and more frequently, hence why you promoted us. Aw, this is great!" expressed Janet.

"Thank you so much, I really appreciate the enthusiasm. I need to be surrounded with people I can trust at a time like this. You guys are in charge of keeping us afloat while I'm at home playing husband and dad."

"I'm proud of you, Foss. As a man, finding a woman that you feel you can spend the rest of your life with is a big deal and something I'm still waiting for. I definitely need to take you out for a drink when you're free," said Ray as he shook my hand.

"Thanks man, anytime. I'm gonna let you both get on with work now, but I just wanted you to know where you stood so far. You're both doing a great job and remember all you can do is your best, so if there is anything you need, please don't hesitate to contact me. The key is to meet each other halfway."

"We won't let you down, Foss," smiled Janet as they left.

I was proud of myself too. I came from nothing to become something and now had loyal people working for me. I built my dreams and every time I think about the struggle, I feel even better knowing that I made it. With a great mind and a blueprint, I made it.

*****

I arrived at the airport and called Justin to let him know I was outside. I'd reached his voicemail three times before I decided to get out of the car and find out where he was. It was 5.30pm so he would have had enough time to check out and at least answer my phone calls.

"Hi, I'm waiting to pick up a friend. He flew in from Las Vegas and was meant to be on the four o'clock flight that landed. I just wanted to know if he was actually on that flight," I asked the help desk.

"Do you know their full name?" asked the attendant politely.

"Justin Paine."

It was a moment before she looked up at me.

"Sir, it appears that he didn't get on his flight this morning. We can provide you with the details of the hotel he checked into if that is any consolation," she suggested.

"Thank you, that would be great," I replied as I tried to compose myself.

Justin would have never missed his flight, no matter how wrecked he was over the weekend. He had a secure job now and wouldn't risk losing it after what we'd been through. I took the details down and went to sit in the car. I was convinced that there was a perfectly valid reason for the mix-up and that he'd be on the next flight down. I drove home and decided that I'd call him back in a couple hours and see if he had landed. If I still couldn't reach him, then I would call the hotel that he had been staying in. When I got back home, Tina wasn't in and the silence forced me into worry. I tried to make myself comfortable but I felt the urge to call Justin again. There was still no answer, so the next best thing was to leave a crude voicemail.

"Justin, pick up the fucking phone! I'm doing you a favour and you're messing me about. I don't have time for this, so when you get this message make sure you call me back."

As time went by, the wave of distress that had come over me was getting worse. I threw the phone across the room in frustration as I knew something wasn't right. I couldn't help but let the negative thoughts creep into my mind. Did he get too drunk? Was he so irresponsible that he couldn't even make it home? Tina then strolled in, somewhat saving me from self destruction.

"Well I know that look Foss, what's happening?"

"Justin was due back from Vegas today, but when I went to pick him up after work I found out that he wasn't on his flight. I've been phoning him since I've been back and still haven't been able to get through. This isn't like Justin, T, and I hate to admit it but I'm worried," I explained.

"Calm down, you probably don't have anything to worry about. You know what Vegas is like. People most likely miss their flights all the time because they're too hungover to make it to the airport on time. Call the hotel where he's staying. When you speak to him and realise that he's alright, you'll regret getting so worked up," she said, trying to reassure me.

"I suppose that's the best and only option I have left right now," I replied as I put my battered phone back together.

As the phone continuously rang, I didn't know what to expect. Imagine Justin was perfectly fine and I really was overreacting. I would have looked and felt so silly, but could you blame me? Nothing was what it seemed anymore since the robbery. It wasn't too long ago that a supernatural force, we still didn't know of, nearly wiped us all out due to our stupidity. To put my mind at ease, I needed to know if everything was how it should be.

"Hello and welcome to the Sapphire Hotel. How may I help you?" answered the receptionist.

"Hello, this is Mr Franklin. I'm calling to speak to a friend staying at your hotel. His name is Justin Paine and the matter is of the utmost urgency," I said.

As she was looking up his details, I looked at Tina.

"Keep calm until you have a reason not to be," she whispered before leaving the room.

"Sir, Justin Paine was taken to the hospital this morning after being found unconscious in his hotel room. We haven't received any updates on his condition, but alternatively we have the number for the local hospital if you would like to give them a call for more information," she explained with a hint of sympathy.

"Thank you," I replied, before hanging up. "See T, I knew it! I knew Justin wouldn't miss his flight," I shouted.

"What did the hotel say?"

"They found Justin unconscious in his hotel room. He's been taken to hospital but they don't know anything else about his current condition. They gave me the number for the hospital he might be in, but part of me doesn't even want to find out what's going on. I honestly can't handle any more losses Tina," I sighed.

I knew that when I went on one of my rants Tina didn't know what to do or say, but everything she did and said made all the difference. She poured me a drink and sat next to me.

"You have been worrying about this like a mad man and now you have the opportunity to find out what's going on, you're stalling. Call them now," she said seriously.

"I'm gonna have to, but it's what I'm gonna hear which is the problem."

I dialled the number and hoped for the best. That's all I felt I could do at that point.

"Hi, I'm calling to query about a friend who may have been admitted early this morning from the Sapphire Hotel. His name is Justin Paine and I wanted to know how he was if he is there."

"Do you know what was wrong with him?" the receptionist asked as she typed in the background.

"I was told by the hotel that he was found unconscious in his hotel room, but I'm not sure what was wrong with him. He seemed fine the last time I had spoken to him and has no previous incidents of illness to my knowledge."

I tried to be as helpful as I could, but the line went quiet for sometime until I assumed we'd lost connection.

"Hello!" I said with raised intonation.

"Sorry for the delay, Sir. We have had a Justin Paine admitted this morning, but I'll have to get the doctor who is treating him to speak to you. What is your name?" she replied softly.

"Foss Franklin."

The next two minutes were gut-wrenching. A million and

one things went through my mind that made me sink that little bit lower. When the doctor came on the phone, I braced myself for the worst.

"Hello Mr Franklin, this is Dr Carter here. How can I help you today?" he said calmly.

His tone seemed a bit too calm for my liking. It seemed as if he had prepared to talk as calmly as he could. I knew I was being over analytical but I just wanted to talk to Justin. I could already hear his voice and his fabricated laugh.

"Hi, I'm calling about a friend, Justin Paine, who was admitted this morning according to the receptionist. Would it be possible to speak to him please?" I said clearly.

A huge sigh swept my words away.

"Mr Franklin, Justin died two hours ago from the disease syphilis."

I refused to believe that they had the correct Justin. Justin didn't have syphilis.

"I'm sure there must be a mistake," I replied in denial.

"Mr Franklin, he is the only Justin Paine that has been admitted into the hospital today. He was found unconscious in his room and was brought in this morning," he added.

"He could not have died of syphilis. It just can't be right. I had spoken to him before he left and he was perfectly fine. Fair enough, I can admit that he was a promiscuous guy, but he was cautious at the same time. He's one of my best friends. I know he did not have syphilis," I protested.

"He may have been in the latent stages of the disease, meaning symptoms are often difficult to detect. However, upon evaluation of Mr Paine's body, I found penile syphilis sores, which is a strong indication of the disease. A blood test will confirm this," he replied.

It was so hard to take in.

"I don't understand. He was fine, absolutely fine," I replied, trailing into disbelief.

Tina took the phone from my shaking hand.

"Thank you, but we'll have to call back at a better time. As you can imagine, this is a really upsetting time for us at the moment. My partner needs some time to come to terms with what he has been told," she said before hanging up and giving me a hug.

"Tina, he was fine. I would have known if something wasn't right. He would have known something was right himself," I expressed sadly.

"Foss, I am so sorry. Maybe he's had the disease for a while and didn't even know. The doctor said it would have been difficult to notice symptoms," she replied.

"Justin isn't stupid. He would always use protection and gets a check-up regularly. I know these things the same way I would have known if he had syphilis."

And then it suddenly dawned on me. It wasn't over. It was never over.

*****

There was nothing to say. Justin was gone and it was real. I woke up at 4am wondering why I was awake. I knew it was late but I called Deano. He still didn't know and I thought it was only right that he knew the news and it came from me.

"Deans, did I wake you up?" I whispered firmly.

"It's four in the morning Foss, what do you think?" he groaned.

"Justin's dead, Deans," I replied.

"What are you on about, Foss?" he replied, perking up a little more.

"He didn't come back from Vegas. He's dead and the doctors say it's syphilis,"

"No! Explain. What happened? I thought he was in Vegas for the weekend at a bachelor party," he replied, now fully awake.

"He was. I went to the airport to pick him up today and he didn't show. I knew it wasn't like him to miss his flight, so I got the details for his hotel and phoned them. They then passed me onto the hospital who told me that Justin was admitted in the morning and died of syphilis not long before I called," I explained.

"Justin didn't have syphilis though. There must have been a mistake, so you need to call them back and tell them," replied Deano aggressively.

"Deano, it was him. I know it was. He's not here and a Justin Paine is dead in Vegas. It's not rocket science when you put two and two together," I responded.

"How did they know it was syphilis? It would take a while for test results to come through, so how are they so sure? We would have known, Foss. Listen to me, I know Justin was careful when it came to women – we both know," he replied, beginning his own process of denial.

"Don't you think I know that too? The doctor explained to me that he found penile syphilis sores but they're waiting for test results to confirm that it is the disease. Not that it matters because it doesn't bring him back," I said, feeling lower than ever.

I didn't want to say what I was about to say, but it had to be said.

"It's coming back for us, Deano. That's the only way this all makes sense. We both know that Justin didn't contract syphilis from a woman, but he was diagnosed with it. We thought we put everything behind us when we turned our lives around because that's what we thought was necessary, but whatever it is doesn't want us to experience a change of heart. It wants us to suffer," I said, staring blankly into space.

"I don't agree. It doesn't fit in with the pattern. Look how long it's been since the robbery and the death of the guys. It's inconsistent and I think you're back to reading too much into things when we've let it go. Don't get me wrong, I don't know how Justin contracted the disease, but I know it has nothing to do with us. Nothing," he replied firmly.

At first I thought Deano was looking at things logically and making sense, but I then got the impression that he was only trying to relieve himself of the guilt. If the robbery is related to Justin's death, then Deano knew that he would primarily be responsible.

"How are you so sure, Deano? We don't even know what it is that put us through this in the first place. We don't know what it's capable of," I replied sternly.

"You've got a beautiful woman by your side, a successful business going and a promising future. If that was going to be taken away in the same way Mason and the others were, then it would be gone Foss. Enjoy what you have. Tomorrow we'll go around to Justin's Foster Mum's house and find out where we go from here, but right now I think we both need to sleep off the shock. I'll call you in the afternoon," he said collectively.

I didn't want to argue with him and wake Tina up, so I complied. We needed each other now.

"Alright, are you good?" I asked.

"I'm good, don't worry about me."

I threw my phone down on the bed and held my head tightly in my palms. I had let it go and brought it all back up again, but it made sense to me. If we were convinced Justin didn't have syphilis, then what else could have killed him?

★★★★★

Seeing Justin's Foster Mum was the worst part of the ordeal. They weren't as close as they used to be, but they still meant a lot to each other. She didn't try to put on a brave face. She didn't try to make out like everything was okay. She was just blank. Justin and Mariam may not have been blood related, but she took him in under her wing when he had nobody and he loved her like his biological mother. It all became too much for me and I left Deano at the gathering to bear the brunt of it all. As I walked back into my comfort zone of a home, the blissful smell of Tina's cooking aroused my senses.

"What are you cooking up in there?" I asked with a faint smile.

"A tasty but healthy stir fry. Here, have a taste," she offered.

"Mm smells and tastes good," I complimented.

"Thank you. I thought with all this going on, a nice meal fit for a king would put that spark back into you," she smiled. "How did today go?"

I sighed as I sat down. "Tina, it was horrible. I've never felt so much sadness in one room before. Especially because we all had mutual friends that we see at each and every funeral, sharing the same hurt we're feeling. It was too overwhelming so I came back early," I replied.

"Never mind, at least you went and showed your face. Now, why don't you change into something more comfortable and enjoy this food," she said.

"Alright T, I'll be back in a bit."

I believed that after a hot shower and a mini dinner date with my woman, I'd start to feel better. A shower always made me feel brand new. The dirt of the day going down the drain to me was like all the negativity being washed away. I've made life-changing decisions under the steaming water that has brought me both highs and lows, but lately the stress had begun to stick. The sadness wasn't fading. I felt like I didn't know what I was feeling anymore. I finished up in the bathroom and made my way into the bedroom, when I caught something at the corner of my eye lying in the middle of the bed. I picked it up and it was the black pouch of stones I had taken from the abandoned house. I looked at the door to see if Tina was still in the kitchen and she was. *Why would she put them on the bed and then go back into the kitchen?* I picked it up and it felt empty.

"Something isn't right," I said aloud.

"Say that again," shouted Tina.

"Not you, I was talking to myself," I replied slowly.

I was still trying to figure out how the pouch had appeared out of nowhere. I opened it up and two stones fell out. I sat on the edge of my bed and thought heavily. It was as if I was experiencing some sort of déjà vu. I could have sworn something like this had happened before: the pouch being in a place where I hadn't put it. To my knowledge it had never left the house, yet five of the coloured stones were missing. I was struggling to piece together all the inconsistencies when it suddenly struck me. Mason, Anthony, Rylo, Damian and

Justin were dead. The orange, green, red, light blue and blue stones were missing from the pouch. The pouch was always turning up in random places with no explanation. The only conclusion I could come to was that each stone missing represented each friend lost. A surge of anxiety came over me and I ran into the bathroom to throw up. The more I pieced together the puzzle, the more fearful I became. The pouch of stones must have been a warning from the beginning. I remembered when it was Mason's funeral and I noticed the orange stone was missing. It was coming back to me bit by bit, which made me feel sick for not noticing sooner. Tina ran into the bathroom and rubbed my back as I heaved over the toilet seat.

"Foss, what's wrong? Don't tell me that bit of stir fry didn't agree with you," she said, believing she was responsible.

"It's all been my fault, Tina. From the beginning we targeted Deano, but it was me. The problem wasn't the money or the drugs we stole – it was the stones," I replied as I washed my face.

"You've lost me. What was your fault? And what stones are you on about? If this is about Justin, then there's nothing you could have done to save him. These things can turn up out of the blue and you wouldn't even know it. You've been to hell and back losing your friends and I know it seems like every time you make progress you're dragged back, but you have to get a firm grip on life and keep going," she said, comforting me.

"That's the thing though, T. I could have saved him. If only I hadn't taken that pouch of stones."

Tina deserved to know the complete story. If I could have hidden it from her I would, but things were escalating to a point of no control. I could be here and gone the next. Just imagining what that would do to her made me realise it was time to open up about everything. Even though she knew about the robbery and had forgiven me for it, I knew this wouldn't be taken lightly. All I could do was hope that she would partly understand, but it wasn't easy telling anyone that something beyond humanity was planning to kill us – let alone your other half. I sat her down with the pouch in my hand.

"Foss, what the hell is going on? Your behaviour is starting to scare me now," said Tina.

"Remember when the guys and I did that robbery that brought so much drama? Well this is why," I said, taking the remaining two stones out of the pouch. "I took this from the abandoned house as a little keepsake alongside the money and drugs we had found. It was as if I was drawn to it, Tina. I didn't think anything of it. I knew they probably weren't worth much, so I kept them around. When Mason died, I remember wanting to throw the orange stone into his grave knowing that it was his favourite colour, but it had gone. I assumed it had got lost in my room and left it at that. There were seven stones in this pouch to begin with and now there's only two. There were seven friends to begin with and now there's only two, Deano and me. I believe the stones are linked to the deaths that have occurred and that because I didn't return them when we brought everything back to the abandoned house is the reason why Justin is dead," I explained meticulously.

As I spoke, I had to analyse what I was saying. I needed to understand what I was talking about if I expected Tina to.

"You know what Foss, I'm tired of this now. We're going

back to the same theory that my brother and the rest of your friends were murdered after you made it out to me that you had let that thought go. I can't handle you bringing this all up again," she sighed heavily.

"To be honest Tina, I don't expect you to understand and I don't think their deaths can even be classed as murder. Not if something inexplicable is involved."

"And why can it not be explained? You really need to deliver this punchline now because I'm becoming frustrated. You ruin a nice evening to rant on about things we've already gone over. You're talking in riddles and I can't stand it. You have something to say and you're beating around the bush when I'm here to listen," she replied.

"What if something supernatural, a demon or ghost, had something to do with what's been happening? Don't freak out, but it makes sense Tina. Look at things with an open mind. As another one dies, another stone vanishes. Where do they disappear to? At first we put it down to karma for taking what didn't belong to us and thought that changing the way we were for the better was what we were being encouraged to do. It's clear now that these stones play a significant part in what has been going on and I need to find out how," I said, painting a vivid image.

"You're making sense, but you need to slow down and process what you're saying. I've had time to come to terms with Mason's death so it's easier for me to talk about it now, but if you feel so strongly about this, then I think the only option is for you and Deano to go back to that abandoned house and return the pouch from where you took it from. It will finally put your mind at rest and we can move on from this for the last time," she replied, sounding so drained.

My paranoia was taking its toll on her again and I wasn't going to jeopardise what I had for a second time. It was time for Deano and me to finish what we had both started.

CHAPTER TEN

Deano and I looked at each other in silence. We didn't want to go back there. That house had already caused so much grief as it was, but I needed answers. If I was going back in there, I was leaving with an explanation. It had been a week since Justin's death and it was still an open wound that stung.

"How are we going about this tonight?" asked Deano reluctantly.

"I would say we go back, return the pouch with what stones are left and at least try to look for some answers – but as we both know, nothing is that simple. Nothing to do with that place has been simple," I sighed.

"I'm tired of running and I don't even know what I'm running from."

"I feel the same way but we need to work this out. Tina and I are engaged and trying for a baby now, so I have to be here. I can't let this get the best of me anymore and neither can you. Let's get dressed and go. Every time we plan, nothing goes to plan. This time we just have to adapt and improvise when we get there," I replied.

We had become entangled in something deep due to our own personal demons and now we were paying the price. The demons were getting stronger and our minds were becoming weaker. Deano and I were both at the point of desperation. It wasn't long before we were again in blacked-out attire, driving back to the death trap. It was like déjà vu all over again as we pulled up outside and I felt the adrenaline rush hit me. Now we were searching for answers, we didn't know what to expect when we went inside, but it was the last card we had to draw.

"I doubt we'll be seen, but take caution with the flashlight anyway," I said to Deano as we ran up to the door we'd entered twice already.

"We're not splitting up, Foss. We don't know what might happen," objected Deano.

"We'd cover more area that way, Deano. Look for anything that may give us a clue as to what and why this is happening. There has to be something. We don't want to be in here any longer than we have to," I explained quietly.

"Alright, but shout me if you need me. I don't care if we get caught as long as we're alive," he replied.

The darkness allowed me to avoid the look on his face as he turned and walked towards what used to be a living room. I switched on my flashlight and slowly made my way up the stairs. With every step was another dreadful creek, but I refused to let fear consume me again. I made a right at the top of the stairs and entered what appeared to be a bedroom. Instantly as I stepped in, I felt awkward as if I was being intrusive and something wanted me to leave. Remembering that I wasn't going to let fear get the best of me, I continued to look around. Deano's loud shuffling downstairs was like music to my ears – knowing he was moving around and I wasn't alone. I started moving things and noticed that many of them were broken. It would make sense with the house being abandoned for so long, but many things appeared to have been thrown around in search for something. The house seemed like it had been burgled before us. That's when a flicker caught the corner of my eye and I spun around startled.

"Deano, come up here now!" I called as my heart raced.

The creaking of the stairs as he made his way up added to the disturbance I was already feeling.

"What happened? Did you find something?" he asked as he tried to catch his breath.

"No but something flickered over there, so I guess that's our next port of call," I pointed.

We both looked at each other waiting for the other to make the first move. In the end, I pulled myself together and started moving things aside. I hated to admit it but I was scared. Usually men could come to terms with anything in due time, but this was something else. There were no terms to come to. As I picked things up, Deano looked for where the light could have come from.

"There's nothing here, Foss," replied Deano, dripping with sweat.

"I'm not going blind Deano, I know I saw something," I said, kicking a box in frustration.

A frame of some sort slid across the floor face down. I walked over and picked up the dusty frame.

"What is it?" asked Deano.

"I don't know, give me a minute."

I blew off the dust and could make out some wording, but the dirt was caked on so much that I couldn't read any of it clearly.

Deano used the end of his sleeve to rub the frame thoroughly.

"Why did you even pick it up? We need to hurry up and

get out of here. There's no time to admire things," he whispered firmly

"I don't know. I kicked the box and it flew out, so I thought I'd take a look."

I turned the frame face up and the stones that were missing from the pouch glistened back at me. I quickly flipped it back over and the stubborn dust was completely gone. That's all there was, seven simple words represented by seven simple stones.

"Deano, look," I said quietly.

"What does it say?"

"It's a list of the seven deadly sins. It begins with gluttony, then envy, anger, sloth, lust, greed and pride," I replied, slightly baffled.

"What do you think it means? Do you think it's what we've been looking for?"

"We don't know what we're looking for, but there's five stones encased in this frame and five of us are dead. This is too creepy to be a coincidence. And how did the stones get back here on their own? The sins must be the link. We committed the robbery for our own personal gain to fuel our own personal sin. Mason died first from an overdose. That must represent the sin gluttony," I explained, astounded at the sense I was making.

Still, I couldn't believe what I was saying myself, even though it sounded legitimate. It was too much to comprehend when we were on edge the way we were.

"So, you're trying to say we're going to die in the order of the sins written on here? No, Foss. This is just a shitty frame you found and you're making it more than it is like you often do. Fair enough I don't know how the stones could have got back here on their own, but that's not our problem now. Leave the remaining stones and let's get out of here. There's nothing for us," replied Deano, rejecting what I had said completely.

"Deano, the stones didn't just grow legs and run here from my house. And why are the seven deadly sins listed on the back? Think about it. Anthony had always been jealous of us and the amount of attention we got. He was the second to die and envy is second on the list. Not to mention how he died. He goes to have his skincare treatment to improve his appearance and dies of septicaemia. Can't you fucking see the picture I'm painting or do you just choose not to see? The guys died a death related to their deepest sin. Rylo gets attacked and beaten to a pulp because his deepest sin was anger. This was all a test. A test for what I don't know, but we need to leave these two stones behind with the hope that we've swerved the death pattern," I replied, giving him the pouch. "Hide the pouch and the frame well under some stuff over there. I want to make sure we're the last to be lured into this trap."

"I don't like where you're going with this, but I suppose it's the only logical explanation we have. Shift those boxes back and let's go. This shit is too much. The more we find out, the more I can't take all the pressure," he said, conceding defeat.

I was angry at myself for not noticing the connections from the beginning. I mean, who would leave all that money and drugs behind? But it must have been left there by someone or something to attract us in the first place. When Deano discovered it, I should have set the score there and then and said we shouldn't get involved. Even if I did, I was the one that had stolen the stones, which made the situation even worse. Justin and the syphilis should have done it for me. I knew that he didn't have any such disease before he had left, but I still didn't understand the reason for all the trouble. All of this couldn't have been brought on by a simple robbery when we had returned most of what we had taken. There must have been more to it.

★★★★★

As we drove back to my house, the confusion of mine and Deano's chatter was starting to give me a headache. Ever since the twister began, I'd felt my health deteriorating slowly. The stress was intense and I could have sworn I saw grey hairs budding. I was convinced that the seven deadly sins were central to all the events that had occurred, but Deano was still sceptical.

"Why are me and you still here then, Foss? I mean, yeah I've been lying low, but I've still been doing my odd jobs on the side to make a living. And you, you used half of that dirty money to get the gym back on its feet. We may have changed the way we live and act, but we're still the same," he said.

I had to agree with him. We were the same on the inside but that still didn't explain what was happening, so I didn't understand how his point was relevant.

"The two stones remaining were meant for us. The yellow stone represents greed which refers to you and the violet represents pride which refers to me. If we were to die, the stones would find themselves with the others in the frame. But if what I am thinking is right, then returning the last two stones and making the best attempt at turning our lives around might have given us the real second chance we already thought we had," I clarified.

"You know I'm next if this doesn't work. I can't describe to you how it feels knowing that you might die anytime soon," said Deano dejectedly.

"Don't think like that. We've literally done all we could do. It must be over now. When we get inside, make sure you act normal. I don't want Tina worrying about all of this even though she knows where we've been," I said over my shoulder as I opened the door.

"Hey Deano, would you like anything to drink?" she offered politely.

"I'm here too, you know," I joked.

"No thanks Tina, I'm fine," laughed Deano.

"T, we're just gonna be in my room for a quick minute," I said.

"And then I want to show you some pictures of my newly decorated place and you can let me know what you think," added Deano.

"That would be nice. Alright, shove off now. I'm watching a black and white film," she replied, clueless as to what we'd just discovered.

I believed that even a man a mile away could hear how strongly my heart was beating as we headed into the bedroom and closed the door behind us.

"You can't keep lying to her about this, Foss. If something happens to you, she wouldn't know why," said Deano.

"Lying is what fucking got us here in the first place Deano, so please don't talk to me about honesty right now. Besides, I'm not lying to her. She knows everything she needs to know up until tonight," I replied firmly.

I paced around the room, thinking over my theory. Well, it was more than a theory. I was certain I was right about our sins being responsible for our torment, but I had the urge to know more.

"This is all too surreal. It's like being trapped in a dream where waking up is impossible," I said.

"Let's backtrack to your karma theory. We toned things down and we were fine, so why start again when Justin goes away?" he asked.

I sat down next to him with a pondering look on my face.

"I don't know. The only way I can make any kind of link is that he must have indulged in lust to an extent where it made everything start all over again – to finish what had already been started," I replied, making up more of my theory as I went along.

"Okay, let's say that's the case. It still doesn't let us know what the fuck is going on. That's the primary question. We've found out so much, but there's still something missing. And it's the something that would make this clear to us," he shouted in the heat of the moment.

"Keep it down, I don't know if Tina is asleep. Karma does play a part because clearly we're being punished, so as I said there isn't much more we can do except try to turn things around. I'll sell the gym if I have to. I'm ready to start my life with a family and a wife. You need to give up the dirty jobs for good Deano. You can get a job like anyone else. Look how you decorated your own place. Maybe that's the skill you need to tap into. It's time to fix up and get ourselves together," I protested.

"I hear you and that's what I'm planning to do. It's just me and you in this now and we need to keep going for our fallen. After all the chaos, I'll never be able to look at anything the same again. Call it traumatised, but this is one thing that will stick with me forever no matter how my life turns out," he confided.

"I expect that because it's the same for me. Trust me Deano, the same for me."

★★★★★

The following days after going back to the house were filled with dilemmas. Deano wasn't a working man, so finding a 9-5 that would suit his needs was a gruelling task. He found fault with almost everything available and believe me he was spoilt for choice. He had an unrealistic wage figure in his head, which made him reject all my average suggestions. As for the future of my gym, it was clear what I needed to do. I used half of my cut from the robbery to invest in making it so much better than it used to be and I couldn't risk having that against me. Taking the fifty grand back out of the gym was an option, but when I thought about it in depth it could have been interpreted as a cheat tactic. I made the difficult decision that I was going to sell up the gym and donate a substantial amount of money to charity. I felt that my good deed would be seen as a step in the right direction. The only glitches that worried me most were breaking the news to Ray and Janet, as well as telling Tina. They would have so many questions that I feared I wouldn't be able to answer. Everyone knew how much the gym meant to me and it was going to upset a lot of people seeing it go. I waited for Tina to come home from work so I could break the news to her. I wanted to put things in the best way possible because I hated myself for getting her wrapped up in this mess and she still didn't know the half of it.

"Miserable," she said as she kissed my forehead.

"Hey, how was work today?" I asked in an upbeat tone.

"It was okay, nothing special. I went to see Mum on my way back and she invited us round for dinner next week," she replied.

"Ah, that's nice of her. How is she doing?"

"She's seen better days, but she's living. That's the main thing," she replied, joining me on the sofa.

"That's great to hear. Listen, I have a bit of news for you," I said, calmly easing into the delicate conversation.

"When you say that, my heart slightly sinks," she sighed.

"No, it's nothing to worry about. I've just been thinking about something and would like to know how you would feel about it," I replied.

"Oh okay, well hurry up because I've got something to tell you too," she smiled.

"You go first then. My news can wait," I replied, curiously.

"No, tell me what you have to say, then I'll do the same."

I assumed it was good news by the way she was acting, but my mind was much more preoccupied with the fact that I was letting my livelihood go.

"I've decided that I'm going to sell the gym," I said bluntly.

"What's brought this on then?" she replied, sounding deflated.

"I think it's time for a change, that's all. I've had a great journey to the top, but the gym brings back too many memories for me. Memories about the good times me and the lads used to have and all the financial stress I had to go through. I think selling up and making a fresh start would be the best option for the both of us, don't you?" I asked.

"Well I know you wouldn't just decide to sell your dream out of the blue, but if you're happy with the decision, then I'll be right behind you. I just know how much the gym means to you and I don't want you to regret it," she said, seeming concerned.

"I've thought about it properly and I'm sure it's what I want to do. The money will be enough to set us up elsewhere if you wanted and I can help out Justin's Foster Mum financially, now that he's gone. I even wanted to give money to some local charities to try and better the community. I have it all worked out, but your approval matters," I replied.

"I think it's a sound idea if you do, Foss," she said, holding my hand.

I kissed her passionately and remembered why I wanted to spend the rest of my days with her.

"Fill me in on your news now. You seem like you're ready to burst," I said.

She turned around and began rummaging through her bag, before she turned back to me and held up a white stick. It took a moment to register but when I saw the two lines, I knew what it meant.

"I'm pregnant!" she screamed joyfully.

"You're pregnant!" I shouted, lifting her into the air.

It was a beautiful moment; it was *our* beautiful moment.

★★★★★

Things appeared to be falling into place with me. I was going to be a father. I sat up in bed and watched Tina as she slept. She was six weeks gone and even with all the morning sickness and hormonal tantrums, sharing this pregnancy with her was a blessing. I never thought I would ever be in such a position: having feelings for someone in such a strong way and bearing a child with the same individual. She rolled over and her eyes flickered open.

"What you doing up?" she asked croakily.

"I have a habit of randomly waking up in the middle of the night for no apparent reason. I suppose it gives me some alone time with my thoughts. How are you feeling?" I replied, stroking her hair.

"I feel a bit drained, but that's expected. Come and lie back down, you look knackered."

"I will soon. I need a drink first, so you go back to sleep and I'll join you in a moment," I replied, getting out of the bed.

I went into the kitchen and poured myself a large shot of brandy. I was aware that it was much too early to start on the booze, but I figured it would help me sleep. Living in doubt was a difficult thing, but the more time that went by with Deano and I still standing was slowly making me feel more comfortable that we were free. Since returning the stones and discovering that it was our sins that put us in danger, we hadn't experienced any more funny business. It left me that bit more relieved that after all the twists and turns, I finally had something to look forward to and I was going to grab it with both hands.

However, it didn't stop the little voice in the back of my mind reminding me that nothing was certain. Anything could happen. But my purpose now was to raise my child and look after my fiancé in the best possible way. Knowing that one stupid mistake had the potential to steal that away from me made me feel cautious, but even worse, guilty. If Tina had to do it all on her own it would be the worst possible thing that could happen. I had obligations to be there to provide the love and motivation she would want me to give. I took another shot as my mind ended another journey.

As I walked back to bed, the alcohol settled in and I was ready to close my eyes and forget everything for a little while. The next time my eyes opened, Tina was gone. I heard her being sick in the bathroom and my heart went out to her. What women had to go through to bring a child into the world was a complex process that's often not acknowledged. I wanted this as much as she did and I was going to be with her every step of the way, starting with checking if she was okay.

"Are you feeling alright now, sickie?" I joked.

"No, I'm not. I've been sick twice already this morning and I feel hot and flustered. I don't think I'll be able to deal with this for nine months," she fussed, sitting on the bathroom floor.

I helped her up and held her in my arms.

"Of course you can do it, T. I know it's hard but it will get easier, and I'm not just saying that. How about I run a nice hot bath and we have a long talk about what's on your mind? I'm sure you'll feel better once you get things off your chest."

"That sounds lovely. Thank you," she replied, hugging me tighter.

"Okay, you go and put your feet up while I sort things out in here," I said as I helped her sit down.

"Foss, your phone's ringing in the bedroom," she said, shoving me.

I hurried to answer the call in time and heard Deano rambling down the line.

"Deano, I can't make out one word of what you're saying. Slow down and start again."

He always did this when he was excited and each time he

had to repeat everything all over again. It's like his thoughts were moving faster than the words coming out of his mouth.

"I know what's going on. I know what's been happening and you were right all along."

"What do you mean? What is it that I'm right about and how do you know whatever you know?" I asked frantically.

"I can't tell you over the phone. Are you at the gym today?"

"No, I'm with Tina at home. She isn't feeling well today," I replied.

"Is there any chance we could meet up today? We *need* to meet up *today*, Foss," he said in a serious tone.

"I'll do what I have to do here first, then I'll make my way to yours. You better not be dragging me out of my house for rubbish. I won't be too long," I replied.

"Cool. I'll see you when I see you," he said before hanging up.

I didn't know how to feel. Anxiety was beginning to set into my veins and I just wanted to know what he knew. I went back into the bathroom and ran the bath. I wasn't going to leave Tina in her state, but playing it cool was going to be a task. I couldn't have her thinking about anything too negative now she was pregnant. Who knows what kind of effect it could have on the baby? I was hoping that what Deano had found out would be the final fragment needed to move on.

"Is everything alright?" asked Tina in the doorway.

"Yeah, course it is. Come here," I replied, giving her a hug. "No matter what happens, I'm not going anywhere you got it?" I assured her.

"I never said you were," she chuckled.

"I'm just making sure you know."

I looked into her eyes as we undressed in silence and made ourselves comfortable in the hot bubbly water.

"This is sweet. I'm glad we can have me and you time like this," she said, lying back on my chest.

"What's running through your mind at this very moment?" I asked, rubbing her shoulders.

"So many different thoughts at one time, Foss. I know it's probably my hormones acting up, but I can't help but feel that I'll struggle with motherhood. Not because I don't want it, but I have no experience in dealing with children," she replied sadly.

"Don't be silly. Why would you even think that? I suppose it's normal to find having a baby a little scary, but I'm here to help with that."

"It's not easy though. My mum struggled on her own and still did a good job with me and Mason, but I don't know if I have the same strength. Letting our little one down isn't an option for me," she said strongly.

"Never doubt yourself and your ability to be a good mother, Tina. Look at the effect you've had on me. You've changed my whole perspective on the topic of love and family. I doubted that there was anyone out there for me, when really and truly she was closer to home than I thought," I replied. "We'll be a great team, don't worry."

"I know we will," she smiled.

I felt like I was doing my part knowing how she felt about things. It was a big step for the both of us, so it was understandable that she was nervous. Speaking of nervous, my nerves were vibrating. Tina and I made the most of our alone time before getting ready for the day ahead.

"I'm gonna pass by Deano's today and see how he is. It's

just the two of us now, so regular contact feels necessary," I said, intentionally deceiving her.

"That's a nice thought. I'm glad you're changing your attitude towards him now. I'm going out with Mum to do some baby shopping, so if you could pick me up on your way back that would be great," she grinned as she tried to hitch a ride.

"To be honest, I think the walk would do you some good. You're getting a bit chubby around the edges," I laughed.

"Shut it!" she shouted, throwing the pillow in my direction.

"I'm off now anyway. I'll phone you later to see where you've got to. Later," I said, kissing her swiftly.

I quickly got in my car and took a deep breath. Having to act as if you were okay when you were far from it was hard, especially towards Tina. That was the first time I had actually felt like I was slipping back into my old ways and getting even better at it. Making up lies as I went along and believing that I could rise above anything and everything – the only difference being that I had company now. That way the danger didn't scare me anymore, but I had to acknowledge that it was my pride that had caused my downturn and I had to accept that I was just like everyone else. I wasn't a martyr or an icon. I was human like everyone else, just trying to live.

★★★★★

I had been sitting in the car outside Deano's house for twenty minutes and he still hadn't opened the door. I walked up to the door and held the doorbell down.

"Deano, do I have to kick down the door?" I threatened.

"Sorry, I was in the shower," he replied, opening the door half naked.

"Put some clothes on please, I didn't come here to see that," I sniggered.

"My house, my rules," he laughed.

"So what was so urgent that I had to leave my fiancé to come down here?" I asked.

"Let me get dressed and we'll have a drink first," he replied, leaving the room.

I had some idea of what it was about but I didn't want to jump to any conclusions. I figured he had suggested having a drink because he thought I would need it. Tina was the centre of my thoughts and I just wanted the conversation to be over with so I could get back home. Deano came back in the room looking bleak and I knew what I was about to hear wasn't anything welcoming.

"You were right about our sins being the cause of all the drama. I ran into a friend called Tony yesterday and we went down to the pub and had a drink. He's a chubby white man that used to live on my road when the lady from the abandoned house still lived there. We used to be close when I was growing up, so I told him what had happened to us. He didn't seem as shocked as I thought someone would be finding out that something supernatural had tried to kill us. He explained that apparently one evening the woman was burgled by seven men who tied her up and left her to starve after taking thousands of pounds worth of her possessions," described Deano.

"How can someone do that to an elderly woman, let alone any woman?" I said, disgusted by the heartlessness of the men.

"Wait, there's more," he replied. "The woman's body was

found some time later but the men were never tracked down. All the police found out was that they were heavily involved in drug trafficking and assumed that's what they were using the money to fund. A few months after the robbery, seven men were found dead and they were all identified as culprits of the robbery by their fingerprints. Everyone believed the woman's relatives had caught up with them and had taken their revenge, but Tony was a friend of one of the men and found out the truth."

"That would explain why we found money and drugs in the house. They stole thousands of pounds worth of her stuff and were involved in drugs. It does make sense, but how do you know it has anything to do with what we went through after the robbery?" I replied.

"If you look at how each of the men died, they all appear to be accidents or natural causes – just like the ways Mason and the rest died. I did some research and Sam, one of the men involved, died in a car accident that was so bad he could only be identified by his dental records. Rylo was beaten beyond recognition. Their deaths both must have represented anger. And Zach, who used to be a chef before he became overweight and found it difficult to continue his profession, was found in his home with a cheese baguette in his mouth. It was later discovered that he had multiple clogged arteries, which basically means he ate himself to death," explained Deano meticulously.

"His death must represent gluttony," I pondered. "He overdosed on food and Mason overdosed on drink and drugs. It's all coming together now, but I still would like to know what's responsible for all the trouble? Fair enough Tony has shed light on the situation, but there are still bits unanswered for."

"Well I thought I'd ask Tony that too and his response seemed genuine. He strongly believes, and when I say strongly I mean he is 100% convinced, that the woman's spirit fed off the darkest sin of each man and used it to take the human form of a young woman who lures men to the house before starting the cycle all over again. This would explain why I heard about the money and drugs from the mysterious woman that was on the phone outside my house that day. I haven't seen her again since that day Foss," he added.

I didn't know what to make of everything Deano was telling me. Things were a lot bigger than we thought and to know that this all started because of those scumbags murdering a woman for her own things was devastating. The most worrying thing about it was we didn't know how many men had gone through the same experience we had and if there were any survivors. It would have given me a bit more reassurance in terms of knowing Deano and I were safe.

"We must have broken the cycle when we returned the stolen goods and changed the way we were going about life," said Deano elatedly. "What else could explain why we're still alive, and why we're the ones still standing? All seven of those men were dead within months of each other. I'm convinced that this is the end Foss. We can relax now."

"I have to admit I do feel better knowing why it happened and I feel happy it's over for good, but the memories of what happened will still remain. Not to mention that our friends aren't coming back. It still hurts when I see the image of Mason in the club and Rylo in the road when I go to sleep. It still hurts that I didn't find Anthony sooner, so he had more of a chance of being here with us today. It may be over, but if you think about it, our mind has been so preoccupied with saving ourselves that the grieving process is only beginning," I replied gloomily.

"I understand Foss, but eventually you'll be able to leave that all behind. You're about to begin a new life. You're getting married and having a child with the woman of your dreams. Me, well, I have a roof over my head and I'm still living. That's all that matters to me now," he replied.

You could immediately tell that Deano had changed. He didn't bring up the topic of money or his materialistic urges. His main priority was his well-being and in a sense I was proud of him.

"So what are your plans from this day forward then?" I asked.

"Well, I have a few job interviews to attend to, so if all goes well I should be working by the end of the month. I just wanna keep busy, you know. As you said, the memories aren't going anywhere, but I don't want them on my mind all the time. Plus I'm going to be a godfather, so I definitely want to prepare for that role," he replied genuinely.

"That sounds great, Deans. This is probably the first time since everything started that I've felt truly comfortable and the first time you seem completely focused," I smiled.

"Tell me about it. What are you going to do about the gym?" he asked.

Talking about the gym was a sensitive subject for me, but I had to learn to accept the fact that in order for me and Tina to progress, I had to give it up.

"I'm selling up and giving a decent amount of money to charity. I figured it's the least I could do considering it's running on blood money. Its just gonna be painful letting Janet and Ray go. I only just promoted them not too long ago and they'll be torn up, even though I'll make sure they're well looked after," I sighed.

"Wow! I never thought the day would come where you'd tell me that the gym will be no more," replied Deano in disbelief.

"Sometimes you have to make sacrifices for what matters most and that's Tina and the baby now," I replied.

"Well, this is something you have to handle on your own, but I'm here when and if you need me. When are you planning to break the news to your staff?"

"The sooner the better really. I'll go in tomorrow to let Ray and Janet know, then they can handle things from there. I don't think I can deal with the tears my decision is most likely to bring," I sighed once more.

"They're just going to have to accept that circumstances change and these things happen," replied Deano.

"Yeah I know, but it doesn't make me feel any better doing it. I'm beginning my new life at the expense of ruining others. Anyway this is starting to get depressing, so I'm gonna head back home and see how Tina is holding up. And thank you. If it wasn't for you bumping into Tony, I'd still be in the dark wondering if I'm going to drop down tomorrow. We're finally back," I said with a gesture.

"Yes, Foss. We're back."

★★★★★

Tina had fallen asleep in my arms and all I could do was smile to myself. I was feeling over the moon inside and out, and I loved it. I had my life back and it didn't feel like I was just saying it. It felt real this time round. Even though at first I was a bit sceptical that Deano could have found all this out, no matter how hard I tried to find a flaw or loophole in the explanation of what happened to us, I couldn't. Everything he had said the previous men had gone through had exactly the same features as what we had experienced. It burned me to know what that woman had had to endure as those scumbags raided her house and left her for dead. I couldn't blame her for wanting to get revenge, which I believed explained why I felt calmer than I thought I would. I understood that the stones were just a sign to lead us to the truth. The whole robbery itself was a trap and in a weird way that somewhat put my mind at ease; me taking the stones hadn't caused the shambles that had weighed so heavily over me for so long. The feeling of guilt was a terrible thing. It torments you regardless of how hard you try to push it out. But I was myself again. I was Foss Franklin with a new vision.

"Aren't you meant to be getting ready for work?" said Tina, jumping out of her sleep.

"Yeah, I'm heading in soon, just thought I'd get a little time with you before I left. You could say I'm stalling when you really look at it," I replied, rubbing her small bump.

"We've been through this and you have to stop feeling bad for changing the route of your life," she replied.

"I know, so let's not go through it again. You go lie down and I'll grab you something to eat on the way back home," I said, kissing her forehead.

"Thanks. Mum's coming over today so she'll be here when you get back," "And Foss, don't worry. You're doing the right thing," she added before retreating to the bedroom.

When I arrived at the gym, I took a moment to sit outside the entrance in the car and watch life go by; to watch the smiling but determined faces go in and the sweaty but fulfilled individuals walk out. I was going to miss it so much – more than anything I've ever had to let go. I made my way inside with a fabricated smile pasted on my face.

"Good afternoon, Foss. How are you today?" asked Janet from the reception area.

"I'm not all that great, I'm afraid. Can I speak with you and Ray in my office please?" I replied rather bluntly.

"Sure, we'll be right behind you," she replied, oblivious to my intentions.

Soon after, the two most important and most trusted employees I'd ever had were sitting in front of me wondering what they were about to be told. My soul sunk as I began to speak. "I regret to inform you that I've taken the decision to put the gym up for sale," I said.

"What? Why?" emphasised Ray.

"I've been thinking about it and I have come to the conclusion that a new start is what Tina and I need. That can't be done when I still own and run this place."

"I have to disagree," interrupted Janet. "We've been here from the beginning and seen how you've grown through both thick and thin into the respected businessman you are today. I can't believe for one second that this is what you really want to do."

"It may not be what I want to do, but it has to be done. I don't want us to argue and fall out in any way. I'll make sure you're both well looked after and still maintain my role as a friend, even once my role as boss is over."

"So what does this mean for us and the rest of the staff?" questioned Ray.

"You will all receive a substantial pay out for the length of service you have given. Unfortunately redundancy is the final stage of the process, however I have many contacts in the health and fitness industry that would be grateful to take on such dedicated individuals – if you wanted to continue working in this field. The decision is entirely up to you," I finalised.

"It won't be the same for me," replied Janet.

"But we just have to accept the decision that's been made and be grateful for the time we've had here. I'll surely miss it," intercepted Ray.

"Ah, won't we all. I have to make my family my main priority now. You guys are still young, well younger than me anyway, so take this opportunity to embrace that and maybe get involved in other things," I suggested.

"It's true. I apologise for my outburst, but it was a shock finding out you're selling up and I'll be out of a job. This place is like a second home to me – but putting that aside, I'm happy for you and wish you all the best," smiled Janet weakly. It was clear she was taking the news hard and fighting back the tears. "I need the bathroom. I'll be on the gym floor if I am needed," she said, walking out.

"She's just upset, Foss. You can imagine all the things probably going through her head at once, but she'll be fine. I guess this is it then. What happens now?" asked Ray.

"Well, I would like it if you and Janet could inform the general staff of the news – making it clear that formal letters and documentation will be available in the upcoming weeks, but until then I'm open to any questions," I clarified.

"Understood. I'll get onto that now," he replied briefly before leaving the room.

They weren't happy at all. I knew Janet had gone to cry

her eyes out and Ray had probably said 'Fuck you' in his head a few times, but I was glad the hard part was over and I could put the rest of my plan into action. I realised I couldn't have no income coming in, so I was considering some smart investments and even helping Deano to set up a business of his own if he was serious about working. It was still early days, but now my mind was much clearer, I had so many ideas that I couldn't keep up with anymore. It felt great. Trying to put all negativity from work aside, I went to pick up some food for Tina and looked forward to some family time.

★★★★★

"How is my beautiful Mother-in-law?" I said as I strolled through the front door.

"I'm very well, Son-in-law," she laughed. "Tina was just telling me the plans you had for the wedding. Everything sounds perfect. I can't wait for the day to come," she added with a smile.

"Ah, I'm glad you approve of everything Mum. We both can't wait for the day ourselves. A few more final preparations and Tina will be Mrs Franklin," I beamed.

"I'm sure you'll be happy together. I haven't seen Tina smile so much in a long time. It's a lovely sight," she replied, stroking Tina's hair.

"Did you get me my munchies, Foss?" asked Tina, stretching for my bag.

"Oh yeah, I forgot. Your cravings are burning a hole in my pocket," I sighed humorously.

"Well it takes two to tango, honey," she grinned.

"So Mum, how are things at home?" I asked.

"Well, it's quiet. With Mason gone and Tina living here most of the time now, it's mainly just been about adjusting. It is good to get some peace and quiet though," she replied, looking in Tina's direction.

"Hey, I wasn't loud! I kept my noise in my room most of the time. It was only when Mason started getting on my nerves and we had to argue, but besides that I was an angelic child," Tina replied defensively.

"Oh, is it really? You used to antagonise the boy, Tina – taking things from his room and all that nonsense. Foss, you would never believe the stupid little things they used to fight over. It drove me up the wall," replied Mum.

"All siblings fight from time to time. My brother Ryan and I were close, but when we got on the wrong side of each other, it was as if a war broke out in the house. But all in all, we always made up and became the best of buddies again," I said.

"Yeah, it is true. Mason was always there when Tina needed him, even when she was in the wrong. Not just for Tina, but for me as well. I miss him more everyday," she replied as Tina leaned over to hug her.

"We all do Mum, but that's why we have to live for him. Even though we've lost him, we'll have a new addition to the family soon and we'll never let him forget his uncle," I replied, trying to stay positive.

"That's definitely something that's keeping me going. Now let's open a bottle of bubbly and celebrate this moment. It still hasn't sunk in that I'm going to be a grandma," she said, lively. "Tina mentioned that you're selling your gym. I'm guessing that's a big change for you. Do you have any plans for what you want to do once it's sold?"

"I haven't decided properly yet, but I have a few ideas. I

want to make some smart investments and buy some shares. That way I'll still have some income coming in, but other than that I mainly just want to enjoy having my own family and making some new memories," I replied.

"Now that sounds interesting. It's good you want to make the most of the early days. They get to the age of five and you start thinking 'Why did I put myself in this position?'" she laughed.

"Exactly! This is why I'll cherish every moment we share before they can talk," I replied, grinning. "Alright, let me get that bottle of bubbly, even though poor T will have to have orange juice I'm afraid," I added humorously.

"Shut up, okay! Orange juice will be fine thank you, but wait, let's take a picture together. The first of many," said Tina, setting up the camera.

As we positioned ourselves in front of the camera lens, a wave of joy surged through me. Who would have ever thought that I would have a family again? Feel the feeling I thought I'd never feel again. I wished my mum and Ryan could have been here but even so, I was just so pleased with what I had. I felt like I belonged. I vowed that my child would never have to witness or experience the hardship I had had to go through. And as we closed in and put on a face of contentment, the flash of our future went off and sent me adrift into my dreams.

EIGHTEEN MONTHS LATER

Breathing in the clean air felt refreshing. Moving out of the city was one of the best decisions I made for myself and my family. It had been six months since we'd moved into our new semi-detached, three-bedroom house and thirteen months since Tina and I saw our beautiful son Nickyle for the first time. We were in the prime of our lives and the most significant part was that Tina was my wife now. Our love had finally been set in stone, which made living in our new home an idyllic experience.

After adjusting to our new surroundings, Tina and I had decided that holding a housewarming BBQ would be a great way to make friends with the neighbours and let everyone else know how we were getting on. I had invited Deano to come over and catch up too. We hadn't seen each other in months, since he had started taking his painting and decorating work seriously – for once, he was the one always busy making money. When he arrived, it was great to see him.

"You made it," I said cheerfully as he walked into the garden.

"Of course I made it, I wouldn't have missed this for the

world," replied Deano as we made our usual gesture. "Where's my little soldier Nickyle?" he asked.

"He's inside sleeping at the moment. He has a habit of missing all the action due to being lazy," I joked. "Why don't you get yourself a drink and we'll catch up on what's been going on in a bit. I'm just gonna check how Tina's getting on in the kitchen."

The BBQ was in full swing and it was honestly a wonderful sight seeing faces that I hadn't seen in a while. It was nice how they made the effort to come out here and share the day with us. Tina and Mum were in the kitchen sorting out the food and doing a brilliant job of it.

"Are you two okay in here?" I asked, popping my head around the kitchen door.

"Yeah, we're fine. The food should be out in a minute," replied Mum.

"That's good. More guests are on the way, but Deano has just come and said hi," I informed.

"Aw, that's nice of him to come all this way. Tell him hi and that I'll catch up with him when I'm less busy. Before you go back out, can you run upstairs and check on Nickyle please? He's been out for a while and needs feeding soon," said Tina.

"Cool, I'll go up now and see how he is. If he's still sleeping, I'll wake him up in about an hour to feed him."

"Thank you love," she replied, smiling.

I quickly ran upstairs only to find Nickyle fast asleep in the same position I'd left him in. Sometimes I would stand over his crib for ages just to watch him sleep. He was a blessing. Tina had had complications with the birth and at one point we thought we were going to lose him, but my boy had pulled through and was as healthy as can be. I kissed him gently before making my way back out into the garden.

"So Deans, how have things with you been going? It's been a while since you started working full-time," I asked, joining him on a bench.

"Foss, things have been better than ever. I completed a painting and decorating course, which included a work placement at the end. When my probationary period was over they kept me on and I've been working for them ever since. Not only am I earning good money, but it's doing something I love that makes it so worthwhile," he explained excitedly.

"I was hoping you would say something along those lines because I've had an idea burning inside me for a while now. How would you feel about setting up your own painting and decorating business? I mean you have the skills and the experience now, but another reason I ask is because I would gladly invest in you and help you get set up. I'm proud of the progress you've made and it's about time I show it," I proposed.

"Are you being serious? Foss, don't pull my leg about something like this," he replied in shock.

"I'm dead serious. Since I sold the gym I've made some smart business investments that have really paid off for me and helped me maintain my wealth. I'm always looking to start on a new project and I think helping you get on your feet with your own business is the one most appealing to me. What do you say?"

"I say hell yeah, that's what I say. I can't believe you're offering me such an opportunity like this. Honestly I don't know what else to say besides thank you, thank you so much Foss," Deano replied, hugging me tightly.

"Alright that's enough, I'm struggling to breathe," I joked.

"Sorry, I guess I got a bit carried away, but what do you expect? I'm going into business with my best friend," he beamed.

"Well I'm glad you're interested, but we'll work on that another time. I think we should celebrate our partnership for now," I said, raising a glass.

"Definitely," replied Deano, returning the gesture. "How have you been doing though? Moving house was a big thing for you, but I must admit it looks perfect for the life you're trying to live. You have the space and calm atmosphere you need to think straight."

"Moving was something I'd been considering for a while so when I had the money to finally do it, I didn't waste any time. Tina and Nickyle settled in better than I expected and her mother comes down every weekend to spend some time with us. At first the neighbours didn't really want to socialise with us, but after noticing we weren't gonna be any trouble, they slowly started introducing themselves. We love it here," I said.

"And so you should. It's a beautiful area and it's your home now. Enjoy it in the best way you can," replied Deano. "I know you might find this awkward, but have you heard that the abandoned house has been torn down? It was all over the news that police had received a tip-off that the house was haunted. The media made a big deal out of it, basically causing a moral panic, and they tore it down to keep the peace."

"Yeah, I know all about it because I caused it. I wrote an anonymous letter to authorities talking about the case of the seven men and the link to the abandoned house. I was vague but clear. Somehow it got in the papers and was the talk of the town for a few weeks. I think they tore it down because the talk was starting to get out of hand. Whatever it was, at least it's gone now. No one has to go through what we did ever again," I replied quietly.

"That's a relief. Every time I passed the place, I got the shivers. If I could uproot and move too, I would. Get away from it all. But today is your day, so let's get back to the party and celebrate your new start," Deano grinned.

"You're right. Get us a drink and I'll be back in a minute."

For once, I didn't feel anything when Deano and I spoke about what happened. It was as if it was completely behind me. I was surrounded by the people I loved and I felt loved. As I walked and talked, I ran into Janet and Ray as they were coming into the garden.

"I'm glad you both could make it. How was your journey down here?" I asked, genuinely pleased to see them.

"It was fine – no traffic, so it didn't take too long. The house is lovely by the way," said Janet.

"Thank you. We put a lot of work into it before it looked like this, but we're happy with the outcome. How about you Ray, how have you been doing?" I asked.

"I've been good. I've started my new job at a gym and it's going very well. Thanks for putting in a good word for me," he replied, shaking my hand.

"No need to thank me, you both deserved it. Why don't you both help yourselves to some drinks and I'll be back with you soon."

"We'll see you in a bit," replied Janet as they walked off.

I called everyone outside and stood in the front with Tina and Nickyle. I wanted to make a speech about the way I was feeling. The atmosphere was filled with optimism and I wanted everyone to feel it too.

"First of all I want to thank everyone for coming here today to celebrate my new start in my new home. I've taken some big steps in my life, but I must say this is the biggest. I have a wonderful wife and a blessing of a son to keep me grounded, as well as all your support. For those wondering why I chose to move out of the city, the answer is that I felt it would be better for my physical and mental state. As you all know, me and my close friend Deano have lost a lot in recent times, but now I feel whole again and it really means a lot that you could come and share this moment with me and my family," I said proudly.

I must say that when I finished my speech, I felt like a new person. It was short but sweet. Everyone was so responsive and it made me feel welcome. I could remember when I was too vain to listen to anyone. I did what I wanted to do without any input from others. I always thought that I was right even when I was wrong and it was disgusting looking back on it now. The change in me was so pure. I cherished everything I had and finally learnt to accept that the people that loved me wanted the best for me and I should be embracing that, rather than pushing it away. My past was my past and I had moved on from all the rejections and heartaches. I walked back over to Deano and downed my drink swiftly. The adrenaline was racing through me and I needed another drink to calm my nerves down.

"It was great seeing you up there, man. Honestly having you as a friend is an inspiration and motivational," said Deano.

"Thank you man, I appreciate that. You're on your way there, so don't give up," I replied.

"Foss! Come and say hello to Mariam," shouted Tina from the door.

"I'll be back in one second. Can you do me a big favour? Go down to the cellar and bring up another case of beer for the drinks table? I'm sure it won't be too heavy for you," I laughed as I walked off.

"Alright but I want paying for my labour!" he replied humorously.

I was so overcome by the amount of people I had to socialise with in such a short space of time, that I didn't even realise that Deano still hadn't brought up the beer from the cellar. I walked around the garden and couldn't find him. I assumed he'd left, but I didn't understand why he would. We were having a good time and I didn't sense any tension. I wasn't going to let it get me down, so I went down to the cellar to get the beer myself. The cellar door was open but the light wasn't on.

"Tina, are you down there?" I shouted.

There was no reply. I walked down the steps slowly and clicked on the light. I saw the boxes of beer still stacked up and realised Deano hadn't even come down here. What was wrong with him? I braced myself and picked up the box of beer, but when I turned around, it slipped out of my hand and spewed out all over the floor. I saw Deano. He was hanging from a beam at the other end of the cellar. His lifeless body was swaying as I slowly stepped towards him. His eyes pierced through mine. My words were frozen. For a split second, all I could do was focus on my breathing and stare back. I then quickly snapped back into action and grabbed his legs to get him down.

"Why would you do this Deano?" I cried. "Why did you do this?"

When I finally got him to the floor, I checked his pulse

frantically. I couldn't believe Deano had hung himself in my cellar. He made out like he was in a good place. He was making the necessary steps to live a better life and even I could see that. It all just didn't make sense to me. My efforts to resuscitate him were no use. He was already gone. I turned my back towards the body, held my head in my hands and cried so hard. Tears filled my palms but I couldn't stop. Deano was the last friend I had from the beginning and he was dead now. It was only when I glimpsed to the side slightly that I saw a yellow stone roll from his hand. My facial expression hardened as I crawled over to pick it up and examine it.

"This can't be it. This can't be from the house," I said to myself confused.

I looked at Deano's body lying next to me and hurled in disgust. He didn't change. He was the same thieving bastard he was from the beginning. As I sat in despair, I pieced together what I needed to know. The last time we went to the abandoned house and I told Deano to leave the stones before we left, he never did. Well, he kept his own. I knew he kept it because he thought it was worth something. There was no other reason why you would jeopardise your life for something like that. I suddenly jumped up and my heart began to race. I'd felt the feeling before, the feeling of fear. The same way I felt when we realised that we were being punished because of our sins.

What did this mean for me now? Deano had broken everything we had tried so hard to build by stealing the stone that represented his own death. How sick could someone be? He had been consumed by his greed and that's why he's lying next to me, dead. I couldn't bear the thought of me and my family being dragged into this after the way we'd turned our lives around. How was I going to explain this? I began to feel flustered and I needed air. I needed air or I was going down. In the most disorientated state of mind, I walked through my guests and leaned over the gate at the back of the garden. I began to throw up continuously and my head began to pulsate. I couldn't handle it.

My mind shut down and I hurled over and over again at the thought of Deano's betrayal. Deano had kept the stone that represented his death after everything we went through. How could he do that to himself as well as me? He knew what we had to do and he still couldn't help himself from thinking about himself. I worried about what was to come. Was the woman's spirit coming for me too? Was she going to take my family? Tears streamed down my face as the painful thoughts ran through me. Tina and Nickyle were my world. What if they were taken away and I was left here to suffer their loss? I would rather be buried alive.

I struggled to lift my head up, but when I did I saw a young woman standing directly in front of me on the other side of the road. I looked up properly but still couldn't make out her features through my watery eyes. She was staring at me angrily. I could feel the rage from where I stood. It was as if I could feel her eyes running over me before they stopped, directly in front of mine. When I stood up straight, her face looked distorted, before I watched as it drained away right before me. Her arms and legs literally turned into skin splashed over bone and her cheeks were no more. I rubbed my eyes to confirm what I was seeing and it was really happening. The malnourished figure still stood rigidly in front of me, despite looking like she had just had her insides sucked from her body. I stared back in astonishment before the figure slowly raised its feeble arm and pointed at me. I turned around quickly to see if anyone else was seeing the same thing, but they were all minding their own business. It was then that I knew for definite that it was down to her why Deano was lying dead in my cellar. I turned back around and the hideous figure smiled sharply at me before vanishing, vanishing into thin air.

I knew who it was. I knew she was livid. I knew it wasn't the last I would be seeing of her.